"I've never tried to seduce you—"

The color bleached from Charlotte's face. "—or anyone else," she added hotly.

"No?" Roberto's smile was lazy. "Then what have you been doing ever since we met, *querida*, if not trying to persuade me in a way you were sure I'd find irresistible?"

Her chin lifted. "What happened between us happened naturally. I didn't ask you about the estate the first night for the simple reason that I forgot. Silly, isn't it? I'm usually hyper-efficient. Then yesterday I couldn't bring myself to spoil our day together. I only brought the subject up now because I couldn't go to my father a third time and say I hadn't mentioned it before you left for Brazil."

"Aren't you going to bribe me, Charlotte?" He moved swiftly and caught her by the elbows, his eyes burning into hers. "Is there no gift that you can offer that will tempt me to give you what you want?"

CATHERINE GEORGE was born in Wales, and following her marriage to an engineer, lived eight years in Brazil at a gold mine site, an experience she would later draw upon for her books. It was not until she and her husband returned to England and bought a village post office and general store that she submitted her first book at her husband's encouragement. Now her husband helps manage their household so that Catherine can devote more time to her writing. They have two children, a daughter and a son, who share their mother's love of language and writing.

Books by Catherine George

HARLEQUIN PRESENTS

873—SILENT CRESCENDO
992—THE MARRIAGE BED
1016—LOVE LIES SLEEPING
1065—TOUCH ME IN THE MORNING
1152—VILLAIN OF THE PIECE

HARLEQUIN ROMANCE

2535—RELUCTANT PARAGON
2571—DREAM OF MIDSUMMER
2720—DESIRABLE PROPERTY
2822—THE FOLLY OF LOVING
2924—MAN OF IRON
2942—THIS TIME ROUND

CATHERINE GEORGE

true paradise

Harlequin Books

TORONTO • NEW YORK • LONDON
AMSTERDAM • PARIS • SYDNEY • HAMBURG
STOCKHOLM • ATHENS • TOKYO • MILAN

Harlequin Presents first edition July 1989
ISBN 0-373-11184-3

Original hardcover edition published in 1988
by Mills & Boon Limited

CHAPTER ONE

A WARM breeze played through the yews in the sunlit churchyard, blowing the thin, dark dresses of the women, ruffling the hair of the sober-suited men. Charlotte Mercer hung on grimly to her hat, praying the vicar would get through the burial service as quickly as possible. The melancholy of the occasion made her uneasy, more anxious than ever to get back to her office. Her father's enforced absence from the helm of the Mercer Group meant, inevitably, that her own desk was rapidly disappearing from view under its load of extra work.

Mrs Mercer moved to support her husband as he shifted awkwardly, and Charlotte shot a hostile look at the walking-plaster on her father's broken leg, seeing it as the root cause of all her present irritation. In Charlotte Mercer's opinion, a man nearing his fiftieth birthday had no business to be driving his Ferrari Testarossa too fast up the bends of his own driveway. She listened, unmoved, as her father cursed under his breath in discomfort. She had been following behind in her own car when he crashed, and still had nightmares about it. Next time, she thought bitterly, she would leave him in the wreckage. It would be a long time before she got over the trauma of dragging her father from the ruined Ferrari, terrified the car would explode into flames any second, the way it always happened in films. By some miracle the outcome had been less disastrous, resulting in no more than a broken leg for Jake Mercer and a badly buckled bonnet for the scarlet Ferrari—unless one took into account the demise of two magnolias and the damage to the retaining wall below the tennis court.

'Are you all right, Dad?' Charlotte murmured.

His reply was regrettably explicit. Mrs Mercer hushed him, her eyes scandalised beneath the brim of her elegant hat.

'Remember where we are, Jake!'

'Why the hell doesn't the vicar get a move on,' he muttered, and right on cue the vicar seemed to pick up speed. A gust of wind sent his voice ringing out over the grave as the coffin was lowered into the ground.

'Ashes to ashes, dust to dust....'

Charlotte shivered, watching with interest as a tall, dark man separated from the group of people opposite and let fall a handful of earth on the crimson roses covering the coffin. Her eyes narrowed under the brim of her hat as she realised he must be the grandson, Mrs Presteigne's heir. And he was very attractive; deeply tanned, with close-curling black hair that gleamed in the sun as he stood for moment, head bowed. Charlotte's throat tightened as she saw the look of genuine grief on the stranger's handsome face. She could understand how he must be feeling. She had been quite fond of Mrs Presteigne herself, sorry for the old lady in her long years of loneliness in exile from her native Brazil. It was sad to realise she was gone at last, that now this rather exotic stranger owned Presteigne House and the two hundred or so prime Yorkshire acres that went with it.

Aware that she was staring, Charlotte's colour rose as the man raised his head and looked directly into her eyes across the grave. And instead of looking away quickly, as she knew she should have done, Charlotte looked back steadily as black eyes under thick arching brows locked with hers.

'Chérie.' Mrs Mercer touched her daughter's arm, and Charlotte turned away quickly, relieved to see the funeral party making a move towards the long black limousines waiting near the gate.

'Right. I'm off then,' she said.

Her father frowned. 'We're all supposed to go back to Presteigne House.'

'Two Mercers out of three should do, Dad. I've got masses of work waiting for me.'

Mrs Mercer nodded briskly. 'Go then, Charlotte. We shall make your excuses.'

'Confound this blasted leg,' said Jake Mercer bitterly. 'I'll be back at my desk next week, never fear. God knows what's going on while I'm away. You tell Ben Ackroyd——'

'Calm down, Dad, the Mercer Group won't grind to a halt behind your back! I'll see to it personally.' Charlotte looked her father in the eye. 'It's what you trained me for, remember.'

Her father sighed. 'Aye, happen you're right. But don't stay at the place too late,' he added irritably. 'Can't have you getting ill as well.'

Charlotte hurried to her little car, thankful to get away from the churchyard and the sombre ritual of the burial service. The entire occasion had given her a chilling reminder of her own mortality, and she drove with more than usual care on her way back to the block of offices in Prestleigh where the

Mercer Group had its being. So she had seen the heir at last, she thought, not very pleased with herself. He must have thought she was a right country bumpkin, staring at him like that, but his eyes had taken her by surprise. Very black and very bright, and so very like Mrs Presteigne's. Charlotte sobered as she thought of the old lady that last time, lying like a waxwork against the pillows on her French, sleigh-shaped bed.

Janine Mercer had taken Charlotte with her to Presteigne House occasionally ever since Charlotte had been a small girl. Mrs Mercer had been in the habit of visiting the old lady regularly, sympathising with her in their mutual exile from their native shores to marry the men they loved. But when Mrs Presteigne finally sent for Jake to talk about the sale of the land he had coveted for years, his Janine flatly refused to haggle with the old lady over property just because her husband had a leg in plaster. That, she declared, was the work of someone in the Mercer Group, preferably Charlotte, who was personal assistant to her father.

'You go in your father's place, *chérie*,' she said with decision. 'Otherwise he will go himself, injured as he is. Also I can trust you to use the tact, eh? Unlike your father.'

And Charlotte, unwilling but resigned, had gone to visit the dying woman ten days before. It had been less of an ordeal than expected, and Charlotte had stayed talking with Mrs Presteigne as long as the nurse had allowed. It had been surprisingly easy to talk about herself, as the old lady commanded, easier still to listen to the story of the latter's romantic meeting with Neville Presteigne half a century before in Brazil. And when Charlotte finally took her leave the old lady had chuckled breathlessly over the story of Jacob Mercer's broken leg, and sent him a message which rocketed him to the edge of apoplexy.

'You mean to say she's made the whole shooting-match over to her grandson!' Jake Mercer's red hair almost stood on end as he glared at his daughter.

Charlotte nodded, unmoved. 'You'll have to apply to the heir if you want the land.'

'But God knows how much he'll want for it!'

'Mrs Presteigne said he's a farmer. Perhaps he'll want to work the land himself.'

Jake Mercer groaned at the mere idea. 'Plough up that parkland! Hell's bells, Charlotte—do you think he will?' He let out an explosive sigh. 'You know how set I am on making the place into Prestleigh's first country club. Golf course, swimming-pool, squash, badminton, gymnasiums, the lot. It's perfect for it.' His eyes narrowed calculatingly. 'I'll have a word or two with the lad when he comes. Farmer, eh? Well I never knew a farmer that didn't want cash. Happen he'll be glad to sell.'

Janine had been strongly disapproving. It was not at all *comme il faut* in her opinion to bother a man with such matters when he would be grieving for a loved one.

'Oh, I'll leave it until after the funeral, lass, never fear.' Jake Mercer's sharp blue eyes moved from his wife's attractive face to the equally pleasing one of his daughter. 'And we'll all turn up at the funeral,' he had stated unequivocally, waving his stick at Charlotte as she began to protest. 'You too, my girl. In your best bib and tucker. And afterwards perhaps we can get the lad over here for dinner. You can do something with garlic and herbs and such, Janine. Foreigners like that sort of thing.' Jake Mercer cheered up visibly. 'After an evening looking at the pair of you across the table he'll likely eat out of my hand.'

As Charlotte parked her car outside the offices of the Mercer Group she smiled at the memory of her mother's outraged face, then grew pensive at the thought of another face, one she had never seen before today, and quite definitely the best looking male face she had ever seen in her life.

When she arrived home that evening Charlotte's parents were enjoying a peaceful interlude with her brother. Four-year-old William was the pride and joy of his father's life, not least because his advent had been something of a miracle, a good twenty years or so after Charlotte's, when both Mercers had given up all hope of another child. William's face lit up like a beacon at the sight of his sister. He hurled himself at her, chattering nineteen to the dozen as usual as he proudly displayed the drawing he had made of her in play-school.

'Michèle let go of Nero's lead today, Charlie!' His blue eyes brimmed with mischief.

Mrs Mercer gave a very Gallic shrug. 'Happily the *méchant* Nero did not encounter any sheep. Michèle was hysterical when they returned from their walk.'

'Poor girl!' Charlotte pulled William up on her lap as she sat down. 'Where's that bad dog of yours now, William?'

'Eating his supper. I've had mine.'

'So I see.' Traces of it were visible round William's mouth. Charlotte grinned and scrubbed at them with a tissue. 'Everything go off all right at Presteigne House?' she asked her parents. 'Was the heir nice?'

'Very charming, but not the type to allow a business talk on such a day,' said her mother. 'And, *Deo gratia*, your father for once realised this and did not even try.'

Jake Mercer looked surprisingly unperturbed. 'I'm leaving it to you, Charlotte. You can have a crack at him.'

Charlotte groaned. 'You're not sending me off to Presteigne House again, Dad, surely! It was bad enough having to hound a poor dying old lady. I flatly refuse to start again on her grandson—even if he's willing to see me, which is highly unlikely under the circumstances. Why can't you go? You're fairly mobile now. I'll willingly drive you.'

'It isn't me he wants to see, lass,' said her father blandly. 'It's you.'

Charlotte's jaw dropped, and she turned quickly to her mother for confirmation.

Janine Mercer inclined her smooth dark head, smiling a little. 'It is true, *chérie*. Your father was on the point of asking Monsieur Monteiro to dine with us, but——'

'But he buttonholed me and asked to see *you*,' broke in Jake triumphantly.

'Why?' demanded Charlotte.

'He didn't say. Just asked if you were free tomorrow evening, and of course I said you were.'

'Oh, did you! It just so happens I'm going to a party in Harrogate tomorrow night with Alan Bragg.'

'Cancel it,' commanded her father brusquely. 'The Monteiro chap leaves for Brazil the day after tomorrow and I want this deal in the bag before he goes.'

Charlotte held on to her temper with an effort, conscious that William was looking anxious. 'We'll discuss it later,' she said, and smiled cheerfully at the child. 'Would like me to put you to bed tonight, William? I'm sure poor Michèle needs a rest.'

The little boy scrambled off her knees with alacrity, running to kiss his parents goodnight before dragging Charlotte off by the hand, making voluble decisions between Thomas the Tank Engine and Babar the Elephant as he went.

Later, over her mother's matchless *Poulet Basquaise*, Charlotte returned to the subject of the interview with Mrs Presteigne's grandson.

'I don't want to do it,' she said flatly. 'If he intends selling he'll sell to you as easily as to me. And if he doesn't I don't honestly see what *I* can do about it.'

Jake sighed impatiently as he eyed his daughter's mutinous olive-tinted face. Her oval eyes, tawny like her mother's, glittered with resentment as she ran a distracted hand through hair which Janine Lefèvre's Mediterranean genes had darkened to a copper shade less fiery than the Mercer red. 'Surely to God you can make use of the looks nature blessed you with to soften the lad up, Charlotte. Use your imagination, girl.'

Charlotte breathed in deeply. 'Not content with packing me off to bully poor Mrs Presteigne on her deathbed, I suppose you now want me to seduce her grandson into getting you what you want!'

'Charlotte!' Janine frowned in disapproval. 'Do not say such things.'

'Your mother's right,' said Jake Mercer coldly. 'You've no call to be coarse.'

Charlotte flushed. 'Sorry. But I'm not at all keen on the prospect of an interview with Mr Monteiro. I've had time to think since I was in the churchyard. I've met him before.'

Her mother's eyes widened. 'But of course, *chérie*. You have. I remember now.'

'When was that?' asked Jake, mystified.

'I was eight.' Charlotte helped herself to more chicken, and grinned suddenly at her father. 'Remember me at eight?'

He chuckled. 'A right little Yorkshire pudding!'

'Exactly. *Maman* took me off for one of our visits to Mrs Presteigne, and she had visitors. Her son-in-law and grandson.' Charlotte's eyes kindled at the memory. 'I don't know how old the boy was.'

'About fourteen, *n'est-ce pas*?' Her mother smiled reminiscently. 'I remember the father better. *Très charmant!*'

'I don't remember meeting him. But the boy was gangly and dark and very sulky because he was told to amuse me. He took me out in the garden and pulled my plaits and pinched me black and blue, and called me rude-sounding names in a foreign language.'

Jake Mercer chuckled. 'Well, he speaks good enough English nowadays, but he's still dark, right enough. And I doubt he'll pinch you or pull your hair across the dinner table.'

Charlotte's eyebrows rose. 'You mean I'm invited to dinner?'

'Aye, that's right. He apologised for not taking you out somewhere.'

'It is naturally not *convenable* under the circumstances,' said Janine serenely, spooning strawberry parfait into crystal dishes. 'He assured me personally that both the housekeeper, Mrs Sutton, and Nurse Johnson will be there.'

'Chaperons yet!' Charlotte grinned, then sighed, resigned. 'Oh, all right, I give in. I suppose I'd better give Alan a ring later and tell him I can't go to Harrogate with him.'

'Can't think what you see in the chap,' said Jake flatly. 'You'd do better with Ben Ackroyd.'

'You mean *you'd* do better with Ben Ackroyd.' Charlotte got up. 'I have no intention of getting involved with your second-in-command, Daddy dear, just to satisfy your business ambitions. Alan Bragg may be a mere advertising man, but he's a lot more fun.'

'Fun!' snorted Jake, but his wife shook her head at him reprovingly.

'Now, *chérie*, let the girl alone. She is a good girl, our daughter. Do not push her so hard.'

Jake nodded glumly. 'Sorry, lass,' he said to Charlotte. 'I just want what's best for you.'

'On that one point, at least, we're in total agreement,' she assured him, smiling, and went off to make her apologies to Alan for standing him up yet again in favour of a business appointment. It hardly seemed politic to say she was dining with another man.

Later on, while Charlotte was giving her father the daily rundown on the day at work, the au pair came in to say Charlotte was wanted on the telephone.

'Thanks, Michèle.' Charlotte pushed aside her papers. 'Who is it?'

'A man,' said the girl. 'A Monsieur Monteiro, Charlotte.'

Charlotte made a face at her father. 'Perhaps he wants to call it off!' She went off to the study, laughing at her father's groan.

'Charlotte Mercer,' she said into the instrument.

'Monteiro,' was the response. 'Good evening, Miss Mercer. I trust I do not disturb your dinner.'

Charlotte liked the voice. It was husky, with a stronger accent than his grandmother's. And it matched his looks. 'No, Mr Monteiro.'

'I wish merely to add.my personal invitation to that which I conveyed through your parents.'

'Thank you.' Charlotte nodded approvingly. A stickler for manners, evidently.

'Please forgive the haste, but I leave again soon for Brazil. May I take it that you are free to dine here tomorrow evening?'

'You have some particular reason for wanting to see me?' she asked bluntly.

'I have indeed, Miss Mercer, but I would prefer to discuss it with you in person.'

Charlotte was definitely intrigued. 'Very well, Mr Monteiro. What time shall I come?'

'Would seven-thirty be convenient?'

'Perfectly.'

'Then I shall arrange for a taxi to collect you.'

'Unncessary, Mr Monteiro. I shall drive myself.'

'As you wish. *Até amanha* then. Until tomorrow.'

Charlotte laughed at the open curiosity on her parents' faces when she rejoined them. 'Relax, my darlings, it was just a very well-bred confirmation of his invite. Formal type, isn't he?'

'And none the worse for that,' said Jake. 'Have a drink, love. Put those papers away. You've had enough for today.'

'*Mirabile dictu,*' said his irreverent child, but she accepted a glass of wine with gratitude.

'What will you wear tomorrow night?' asked Mrs Mercer.

Charlotte pretended to give it thought. 'Let's see... Leather mini skirt? Strapless balldress? What do you think he'll fancy?'

Jake scowled. 'Don't be daft. Just wear something pretty, girl—nice and feminine like your mother's clothes.'

'I am six inches taller than *Madame Ma Mère*.' Charlotte smiled at her small, curvaceous mother, who looked far more credible as the mother of young William than of her twenty-four-year-old daughter. 'I'm the tailored type, and Senhor Monteiro will just have to take me as I am.' She stopped, surprised at the look on her father's face.

'This is just a business deal, Charlotte,' he said emphatically. 'You're my representative, nothing more. If the chap steps out of line, walk out. You're more important to me than a few acres of land.'

Charlotte put a hand on his arm, touched. 'Thank you, Dad. Not that I think there's anything to worry about. I'm sure Mr Monteiro will be the perfect gentleman.'

'Of course he will,' said Mrs Mercer matter-of-factly. 'Why else would he ask you first, Jake? Besides, he hasn't met Charlotte yet. His reasons for wanting to see her cannot be personal, *chérie*.'

Whatever reason the Presteigne heir had for wanting to see Charlotte Mercer, she kept very quiet about her own reasons for accepting his invitation. Not for the world would she have wanted her parents to guess that she was motivated by that exchange of looks in the churchyard, that in actual fact wild horses wouldn't have kept her from meeting the handsome Mr Monteiro.

Charlotte was very glad of her father's absence from the Mercer Group next day, since it would have been difficult to conceal the fact that thoughts of the evening ahead kept coming between his personal assistant and her work the entire day, resulting in very uncharacteristic nerves as she parked her car outside the imposing façade of Presteigne House at exactly seven-thirty. To compose herself, she lingered a moment on the balustraded terrace overlooking the beautiful property her father so badly coveted. From where she was standing she could see out over the formal gardens along a yew walk leading to copses of trees and rolling parkland, the serenity of the scene gilded by the sunset light of the August evening. Charlotte sighed. Looking at the place now, it seemed unlikely the new owner would want to sell it. Unless he really needed the money, of course. She fervently hoped so. If he did it would make life a lot easier for everyone who had to live with Jacob Mercer.

Charlotte turned away to ring the bell, and the door under the pillared portico opened at once on the stout figure of Millie Sutton, the housekeeper. Her normally cheerful face looked swollen and pink about the eyelids as she smiled at the tall girl.

'Charlotte, love, come in, come in. How's your Dad's leg? Your mother looked that smart yesterday, but it was a sad occasion. I miss the old lady right badly, you know.'

Charlotte squeezed the woman's hand sympathetically. 'I'm sure you do, Mrs Sutton. I didn't know her that well, of course, but I felt terribly sad myself when she finally died.'

The housekeeper led Charlotte across the large square hall and showed her into a formal drawing-room overlooking the terrace. 'The lad'll be with you directly, Charlotte. He had a phone-call from the solicitor just as you arrived, but he won't be long. Sit down and make yourself comfortable while I see how the dinner's doing'.

Charlotte felt too restless to sit down, remembering other times when she had perched on the little tapestry-covered footstool while her mother and Mrs Presteigne chatted over strong black coffee and little sweet cakes. She strolled over to the tall windows, wondering if the sulky, hostile boy she barely remembered had grown up into a pleasanter man to match his rather spectacular looks. If not, it was likely to be an uncomfortable evening. Not, of course, that she intended to stay long. She would leave the moment dinner was over and her offer tendered on behalf of the Mercer Group. Besides, it was unlikely her host would be feeling very convivial under the present circumstances. She gazed absently at her outline in the window, a tall, slimly-built figure in her black linen suit, the brightness of her hair just discernible above the pale blur of her face in the shadowed glass.

'Forgive me, Miss Mercer,' said a voice from the door. 'I am late. I apologise.'

Charlotte turned slowly to face Mrs Presteigne's grandson. She looked at him in silence as he crossed the room, shocked by a reaction so overpowering, so alien from anything she had ever felt before, that she was frightened. And angry with herself for being frightened. Charlotte Mercer, who loved thunder-storms, air-flights, galloping over the moors on a spirited horse, was a stranger to fear of any kind.

Her host held out his hand and smiled. 'Welcome. I am Roberto Gaspar Monteiro. It was so kind of you to come here tonight.'

Not kind; unwise, thought Charlotte, as she pulled herself together. She took the lean brown hand, dismayed as her heart leapt at the hard, cal-loused touch of it. 'How do you do,' she said. 'Please accept my condolences, Senhor Monteiro. I liked your grandmother very much.'

'And she you, Miss Mercer.' Roberto Monteiro waved a hand towards one of the velvet chaise-longues flanking the marble fireplace. 'What may I offer you to drink?'

Something to calm me down, thought Charlotte, glad to sit. Her knees were trembling. 'Dry sherry, please, Senhor Monteiro.'

Her host turned away to a Chinese lacquer cabinet at the far end of the room, giving Charlotte the chance to study him at leisure. Seen in profile, the lashes fringing his eyes were thick and curling enough to arouse envy in any woman, a sharp contrast to the jut of the nose, which was pure Roman and all male, as was the set of the wide, flexible mouth and the aggressive chin. His shoulders were broad under the sober dark cloth of his suit, and his face and neck darkly tanned, as though he spent his life in the open air. As he would, of course, Charlotte reminded herself. He was a farmer. And if she hadn't known the man had Saxon Presteigne blood in him she would never have guessed. There was no confusion of genes in Roberto Monteiro, as there was with herself. He was all Latin, from his crisply curling black hair to the tips of his toes and the slight swagger in his walk as he crossed the room towards her.

Charlotte took the glass he offered and raised it in toast. 'To Mrs Presteigne,' she said quietly.

His eyes met hers as he inclined his head gravely. 'To my grandmother, Ana Maria Monteiro Presteigne. May she rest in peace.' He drained his glass and set it down on a table beside him as he sat on the sofa facing Charlotte. 'I wish to thank you for coming to her funeral yesterday.'

'The least I could do.'

'I had hoped to see you here afterwards, but your father explained that you were needed at the offices of his company.'

Charlotte nodded, and took a reviving sip of sherry. 'My father's accident has meant extra work for many of us at the Mercer Group, I'm afraid.' She smiled for the first time. 'Not that my father will stay at home much longer, whatever my mother says. Nothing will convince him the firm is functioning properly in his absence.'

Roberto Montiero's strong white teeth gleamed in a smile which quickened Charlotte's pulse. 'And is it?'

'Functioning? In my opinion, yes.'

'And what is your occupation in the Mercer Group?'

'Personal assistant to my father.'

'Do you enjoy what you do?' The bright, black eyes, so like those of Mrs Presteigne, were intent on hers in a way Charlotte found very unsettling, as though he could read her mind, discover that enjoyment was not the precise word for her feelings about her job.

'I'm very fortunate,' she parried. 'Not many girls have a well-paid job waiting for them when they leave college.' It would have been disloyal to her father to tell this stranger that it had never been what she wanted. That Jake Mercer had been adamant that his daughter took a course in business studies instead of letting her go to the art school she yearned for.

'Your father also is fortunate.' Her host rose to refill her glass, and Charlotte took herself firmly in hand, annoyed to feel so shaken by the mere presence of this man in the same room. She took a few calming breaths as the handsome Brazilian returned with their drinks, determined to talk normally, behave in her usual self-possessed way, and ignore the erratic behaviour of her pulse.

'How do you like Yorkshire, Senhor Monteiro?' she asked. 'I imagine its climate is more bracing than in your part of the world.'

'It is beautiful here now, with the sun shining, but in colder weather I find it less *simpático*. I came here in winter the first time when I was a boy.'

'I remember,' said Charlotte without thinking.

Roberto Monteiro leaned forward, his face alight with curiosity. 'How is that?'

'I came to tea with my mother one day while you were here.' Charlotte flushed as an incredulous look of recognition dawned in the black eyes.

'*You* were that little girl I was made to entertain?'

'Entertain! You pinched me, pulled my hair and were insufferably rude!' The words were out before Charlotte could stop them, and he looked taken aback for a moment, then threw back his head and laughed delightedly, just as Mrs Sutton arrived to say dinner was ready.

'That's nice to hear, Roberto,' she said approvingly. 'Your grandmother wouldn't like to see you so glum and grief-stricken as you were at first.'

'Miss Mercer was just reminding me we had met before,' he said, jumping to his feet.

'I was eight, Mrs Sutton,' explained Charlotte ruefully. 'A dumpling with braces on my teeth, and plaits.'

'Well I never,' marvelled the other woman. 'That's right. I remember now. Your father was here as well, wasn't he, Roberto?'

The handsome face sobered. '*Está certo*. It was a long time ago. Many things have happened since then.'

'That's a fact.' The woman smiled sadly. 'Now then, come along and eat this dinner.'

Roberto Monteiro seated his guest with ceremony at a table laid for two on a shining expanse of mahogany that could have accommodated a dozen more settings with room to spare. Charlotte shook out a starched damask napkin, wondering gloomily whether this unfamiliar tension she was experiencing would allow her to eat very much.

'I thought perhaps Mrs Sutton and Nurse Johnson might be dining with us,' she said, as she made a start on the asparagus soup in front of her.

Roberto looked blank. 'Should I have insisted they did that? Would you have felt happier to have them present?'

Charlotte shook her head, 'No, of course not. But my mother made a point of mentioning they were still here.'

The blankness gave way to a comprehending gleam. 'Ah! She would not have allowed you to come here alone otherwise.'

Charlotte smiled demurely, and went on with her soup.

'You have changed a great deal since you were eight years old,' went on Roberto Monteiro. His eyes were frankly appreciative as they moved over her gleaming coils of hair to her face, which was tanned to a gypsy brown by the sun of the previous week or two. 'And I assure you that I have changed much also. You have my oath that I will not pinch you or dare to attack that so perfect hair.'

Charlotte grinned, suddenly more relaxed. 'I'm relieved. It takes quite a time to get it like this.'

He leaned across to fill her glass with pale, sparkling wine. 'The result is worthy of the effort.'

She met his eyes candidly. 'To be honest I wanted to look as well groomed as possible to come here tonight. For confidence, I suppose.' She sipped her wine, startled to find it was champagne, and vintage at that.

His arching black brows rose. 'You were surely not nervous about meeting me?'

'Not nervous exactly. I just couldn't imagine what reason you had for asking me to come here,' she said bluntly.

There was a break in the conversation while Mrs Sutton came in to remove their plates and place a roast sirloin of beef in front of Roberto. Charlotte watched, fascinated, as her host carved with lightning precision, wielding the carving-knife with great skill while the housekeeper rushed to and fro with fresh vegetables from the kitchen garden, and finally a great dish of smoking hot Yorkshire pudding, fresh from the oven.

'Do you like our traditional dish, Senhor Monteiro?' Charlotte smiled at him as she began on her meal.

'Very much. But of course we eat beef a great deal in my country.' He raised his glass *'Saúde.'* He hesitated, then smiled questioningly. 'Could you not call me by my first name? I would be much honoured.'

Charlotte felt her colour rise. 'Yes. If you wish.'

'And you will allow me the privilege of calling you Charlotte? Or do you have another name?'

'Several. My mother is from the Dordogne, and she insisted I was given some Lefèvre family names as well as Charlotte, which was my father's choice. Feminine of Charles, you see; he wanted a son.' Charlotte laid down her knife and fork and sipped her champagne. 'I am Charlotte Héloïse Janine Véronique.'

Roberto's laugh was spontaneous. 'I had not thought to meet a lady with such names in Yorkshire!'

'It was a terrible nuisance when I was in school.' Charlotte returned to her roast beef, but after a while she gave up.

'You are not hungry?' he asked quickly.

She smiled apologetically. 'It's very warm tonight.'

'May I take your jacket? You will be cooler.'

'Thank you.' Charlotte kept her eyes down as she slid out of the tailored black linen with its heavy shoulder pads, grateful to feel the air cool on her bare arms. She felt his fingers brush fleetingly against her skin, and blood rushed to her face as he took her coat out of the room.

For God's sake get a hold of yourself, girl, she thought irritably, and finished the champagne in her glass. She felt a little better, able to smile at Roberto with more equanimity when he returned.

'I know it is not customary to drink champagne with the roast beef, but there were several bottles of Bollinger in the cellar. It seemed a sin to leave them there.' He smiled as he refilled their glasses.

Charlotte was in full agreement. Her father's taste ran to full-bodied red when it came to wine, and it felt pleasantly decadent to drink champagne throughout the meal, regardless of what they were eating.

'You have eaten very little,' observed Roberto, as they sat over coffee later in the faded gilt and velvet formality of the drawing-room.

'We're not accustomed to heat in Prestleigh.' Charlotte shrugged, smiling at her host, who was leaning back relaxed on the chaise opposite, watching her through the curling smoke of a thin black cigar. It was dusk by this time and several lamps gave a soft glow to the room. Roberto Monteiro's skin looked darker than ever above the gleam of his white shirt, and Charlotte wondered when he was going to broach the subject of his reason for asking her here. 'It takes us northerners by surprise.'

'You look as though the sun agrees with *you*, Charlotte.'

'My mother's genes mixed with the Mercer Saxon variety, I suppose.'

'I am curious. May I ask how your parents came to meet?'

'Of course. My father went on holiday to France when he was eighteen or so. He'd won a little money on the football pools,' Charlotte stirred her coffee absently. 'He was a bricklayer on a building site at the time, so when he fell in love with the daughter of the hotel proprietor where he was staying it wasn't very popular with Papa Lefèvre. *Maman*, who was only sixteen, was as mad about Jake Mercer as he was about her, but her parents were adamant. No cash, no Janine.'

Roberto leaned forward, his eyes bright with interest. 'So what did your father do? Did he run off with your mother?'

Charlotte shook her head. 'No fear. He's very straight, you know. He came home and simply set out to make money. And when Dad wants something he doesn't give up until he gets it. He's something of a legend locally. Prestleigh's quite proud of its local hero. Four years from the day he met

Janine Lefèvre he had his own small building firm, with enough money coming in to convince my grandfather that Jake Mercer was a suitable husband for his daughter.' Her smile was whimsical. 'And so they lived happily ever after.'

Roberto nodded approvingly. 'A very romantic story. Very much like my grandparents.'

'Ah, but with a difference. From what your grandmother told me I gather Neville Presteigne possessed sufficient money and breeding to make him eligible to her family from the start.'

'*E verdade*. Do *you* believe in love at first sight, Charlotte?'

If anyone had asked her that only a few days before, Charlotte would have laughed and said no. Now, looking at Roberto Monteiro, she was by no means quite so sure. But then, who was to say if 'love' was an accurate description for the unfamiliar hot and cold shivering feelings which felt suspiciously less cerebral than love, and were situated in a region of her person rather less estimable than her heart?

'I would like to,' she said with caution.

Roberto smiled and rose to his feet. 'Let us drink more champagne.'

Charlotte shook her head. 'I can't. I have to drive back home, remember.'

'Then leave your car here. I shall ring for a taxi.'

She wavered. Why not? He was here for only one night. And no one else was in the habit of plying her with vintage champagne. 'You're very kind. Thank you. I'll send someone to pick up my car tomorrow.'

Roberto's eyes lit with gratifying delight. 'Then if you will excuse me for a moment, Charlotte, I will fetch the champagne, also something else which will explain my reasons for asking you to come here tonight.'

Charlotte watched him walk across the room, shocked to discover how bereft she felt at the prospect of even a few moments' separation from him. This is ridiculous, she told herself sternly, and got up to march over to the windows. If she were sensible she would get herself out of here as fast as she could before she made a complete fool of herself. She squared her shoulders and took in a few deep, calming breaths. She would just wait to hear what Roberto Monteiro had to say, then she would pass on her father's bid for the Presteigne estate, and simply go home. She stared unseeingly at the crimson afterglow edging the sky, trying to come to terms with the preposterous fact that a man she barely knew was likely to leave a great hole in her life when he departed from it.

'You are dreaming,' said the attractive, already familiar voice, and Charlotte jumped yards before turning to face her smiling host.

'I didn't hear you come in. I was miles away.' Charlotte was grateful to the fading light for hiding the sudden colour in her face.

'Come,' he said, taking her by the elbow. 'Let us sit down. I have a little presentation to make to you.'

Charlotte was so shaken by his touch she hardly heard what he was saying. Dazed, she let him lead her back to the lamplit centre of the room, where he sat beside her this time on one of the sofas. He took two leather boxes from his pocket, and laid them beside Charlotte.

'I had only two days with my grandmother before she died,' he said huskily. 'But she was able to talk quite lucidly right up to the—to the end. She spoke much of you and your mother, Charlotte, and made me promise I would give these *lembranças* in person.'

'*Lembranças?*'

He thought for a moment. 'Keepsakes? My grandmother was grateful to the Mercer ladies for taking pity on a lonely old woman. She wished you to have these, Charlotte.' He opened one of the boxes and took out a string of perfectly matched pearls.

Charlotte sat very still, staring at them. 'But I can't—I mean, I never expected . . .' To her intense embarrassment her eyes filled with tears.

'Charlotte, do not weep.' Roberto's voice deepened as he took a handkerchief from his pocket and touched it gently to her eyes. Charlotte dodged away from his touch, unable to bear it, and drew back at once, frowning, as she dried her eyes and looked round her for her handbag.

Roberto retrieved it from the sofa opposite and handed it to her, and Charlotte thanked him gruffly as she rummaged for a tissue, anxious to blot her tears before her mascara could run down her cheeks.

Roberto maintained a tactful silence while she recovered her composure, and Charlotte looked up at him after a time, her eyes doubtful. 'I don't feel I should accept such a valuable keepsake—Roberto.'

He smiled gently. 'It was my grandmother's dying wish.'

Charlotte steeled herself to clear up the question which had been burning inside her all evening. 'Shouldn't your wife have them?'

There was silence for a while, then Roberto Monteiro rose to his feet to pour more wine, his face shuttered. 'You need feel no distress about my wife, Charlotte. Amalha has no need of my grandmother's jewels.'

CHAPTER TWO

HIS wife. The words hit Charlotte like a blow from a hammer. But of course he was married. How could someone as attractive as Roberto Monteiro not be! She pulled herself together forcibly, summoning the composure learned the hard way during the past three years as her father's personal assistant.

'Then if you are sure, thank you,' she said quietly. 'I shall treasure them always.'

'You did not know I had a wife?' he asked.

'I knew nothing about you at all.' Charlotte's hand was commendably steady as she took the glass he handed her. 'I saw more of your grandmother when I was young, before college and my job took up so much of my time. And since William's arrival my mother's visits have been less frequent, too, much to her regret.'

'William?' Roberto seated himself beside her once more, his black eyes questioning.

Charlotte smiled. '*L'enfant du miracle,* my mother calls him. My little brother—four years old and a right little handful.'

His answering smile was warm. 'So William is the youngest of the family?'

'Yes, indeed. He arrived very late on the scene, long after my parents had given up hope of another child.'

'There are others?'

'No. Just William and me, with twenty years between us.' She hesitated. 'Do you have children, Mr Monteiro?'

'Roberto, *faz favor*.'

'Roberto,' she repeated obediently.

'Alas no, I have no children.' He took the pearls from the satin-lined box. 'Let me fasten these around your neck, Charlotte. The catch is a little difficult, I think.'

Charlotte bent her head, feeling the touch of his fingers like a brand on the nape of her neck. A tremor ran through her and Roberto touched the skin of her upper arm in concern.

'You are cold? Shall I tell Millie to turn on the heating?'

'Good heavens, no!' Charlotte moved farther away. 'I'm not in the least cold.' Which was no more than the truth.

Roberto opened the other box to disclose a pair of exquisite pearl drop earrings. 'These are for your mother. Aninha said to give them with her affection and appreciation.'

Charlotte touched the earrings gently. '*Maman* will love them. Your grandmother was very generous.' She smiled into the intent face so near her own, startled by the expression in the thickly fringed eyes, almost sure he was looking at her with ... She looked away quickly, busying herself with putting the jewel-box in her bag. This was becoming unbearable. If she was beginning to imagine things it was high time to take herself off, before she did something really foolish.

'Your hands are shaking,' he said, and she gave him a startled, sidelong glance, heat rising inside her as he leaned closer. 'You are nervous, Charlotte?'

'Nervous?' She managed a little laugh. 'Why should I be nervous?'

Roberto closed the small gap between them and took her hand in his. 'I am not sure. But I am hoping with all my heart that it is because you are alone with me.'

Charlotte tried to tug her hand away, but his hard, tenacious fingers held on to it. 'Mr Monteiro—Roberto—please. Your wife....'

'Is dead,' he said without emotion. 'I have been *viúvo*—widower, for several years.'

Charlotte looked blindly at their joined hands. 'Oh. I'm so very sorry. I had no idea. And I was rattling on about children—forgive me, please.'

'Por nada.' He smiled a little, then frowned as her teeth caught in her lower lip. 'Do not injure your beautiful mouth in that way, Charlotte.'

Kiss it better, then, she almost said, and bit harder on the lip.

'You are a very beautiful lady, Charlotte Mercer,' he said huskily, his hand tightening on hers. 'And I am very glad my grandmother asked me to deliver the *lembranças* to you in person.'

Charlotte turned grave, considering eyes on him. 'Are you?'

'Very glad, and very unsure of myself.' His voice was a little unsteady as he bent nearer still, so near she could see the faint dark shadow on his jawline, breathe in the warm, clean male scent of his skin. 'Because I am very conscious that I must not offend such a person as Miss Charlotte Mercer by speaking on any subject more personal than her health, the

weather, her family.' His voice roughened. 'When
I most wish to tell her how lovely she is, how different from the woman I expected.'

'What did you expect?' she asked in a whisper.

'At the funeral yesterday I saw a very elegant
lady in a black dress, with a hat hiding her face
and hair. I looked, and I could not look away.' His
smile grew whimsical. 'It is strange, is it not? I asked
you here—with great reluctance I admit most
freely—out of duty to my grandmother's wishes.
Deus, how was I to know that one look at you
would change my life?'

Charlotte's heart have a great lurch. 'Change
your life?' she repeated incredulously.

'*E verdade*. I do not lie.'

A knock on the door interrupted them. Roberto
cursed under his breath and moved away to leave
a discreet distance between himself and Charlotte
as Millie Sutton came in to ask if they needed anything before she went to bed. Roberto assured her
nothing more was required of her, and the housekeeper bade them both a pleasant goodnight and
withdrew, leaving a tense silence in the room as the
door closed behind her.

'That was unfortunate!' Roberto leaned forward,
his hands clasped between his knees as he stared
down at the faded roses woven in the carpet.
Charlotte sat back in her corner, her fingers on the
pearls at her throat, her eyes free to follow the way
Roberto Monteiro's crisp, curling hair hugged the
shape of his head.

'Now,' he went on, addressing his shoes, 'you
have gained time to think, to retreat, to convince
yourself that this foreigner must be a fool to tell

you such *fantasias* a mere hour or two after meeting you.'

'I was surprised,' she admitted with caution.

'I spoke the truth.' He kept his eyes down, as if, she thought suddenly, he was afraid to look up and see her reaction. How am I supposed to answer that? she thought wildly. Tell him that *my* life is upside down too? What was the correct procedure under such circumstances? Falling apart at the merest touch of a man's hand was not at all her style. It had always been the men who had kissed *her* and gone to pieces in the process. Never for a moment had she expected to experience any emotion remotely similar for herself. Long seconds ticked by in silence, then Roberto turned his head and looked at her, and a flame leapt in his eyes. He sat motionless, and Charlotte looked back at him very steadily. Their eyes held and fused, and the effect was as electrifying as though their bodies had done the same.

'Charlotte?' Roberto's voice was gruff, unsteady, and he covered the space between them and took her in his arms, and suddenly it was all so uncomplicated. For the few moments left while she was still capable of thought Charlotte wondered why they had been delaying, then Roberto's mouth was on hers. His arms held her in a ravishingly tender embrace, while he kissed her with a passionate concentration that progressed quickly to a shaking, hungry demand. Charlotte answered it unstintingly, with an ardour that sent a tremor through Roberto's muscular frame. His arms crushed her against his chest and she flinched and he drew away a little.

'Forgive me, *carinha*—I have frightened you.'

'No. Your buttons are digging into me.' Charlotte smiled into his dark, intent face, and he breathed in sharply and shrugged off the offending jacket, tearing at his silk tie and tossing it away.

'*Agora,*' he breathed, and took her on to his knees, holding her against his chest. 'Now—it is better?'

It was so very much better that Charlotte closed her eyes and held up her mouth for answer, and Roberto covered it with his own, his arms locked firmly around her waist. He made no move towards more intimate caresses, even though her blouse was a flimsy, wrap-over affair which tied at the waist and would have been easily discarded, but his kisses deepened with mounting demand, and at last he drew away and raised a hand to her head, pressing it gently to his shoulder, his breathing almost agonised as he stroked her hair with an unsteady hand.

'Charlotte, *carinha*—forgive me. At such a time I should not ... It is not my way to—to——'

'To make love to a strange woman?' Charlotte drew back to smile at him, managing to tease a little, and his face cleared.

'I force myself to wait—at least until the second meeting.' His answering smile was dazzling. 'Or shall we say I do not make love to a lady until she wishes me to.'

'And if that happens to be the very moment she meets you?'

'What would you have a man do?' His eyes darkened and he bent his head to kiss her smiling mouth, then drew away resolutely. 'No, no! No more of the kissing.'

'Why not?'

'Because, as I think you must know very well, Miss Charlotte Mercer, I cannot trust myself to go on kissing you without wanting more than the kissing. Much more. You would be angry—and rightly so.'

Charlotte slid off his lap to stand in front of him, smiling ruefully. 'And even more to the point, Senhor Monteiro, you leave here tomorrow.'

Roberto came to his feet in a single, economical movement, and took her hand. 'If I could arrange to stay longer would you spend the time with me, Charlotte?'

She stared up into his imperious face, her mind working furiously. Today was Friday. Which meant a whole weekend to herself. If Roberto Monteiro wanted to stay longer surely she would be a fool not to spend as much time with him as he wanted. It was unlikely the opportunity would ever present itself again.

'Well, Charlotte? Will you?' he said urgently.

She looked down at their joined hands. 'I'm not usually a creature of impulse, Roberto.'

'I believe you.' Gently he raised her face to his. 'Would I be right in thinking you do not allow my sex to disturb that poise of yours? *Está certo?*'

'If you're asking if you're right then yes, you are.' She gave him a crooked little smile. 'I work with men all day long. I see the everyday, irritable, chauvinist side of most of the men I know, which makes it difficult to view them in a softer light outside working hours.'

Roberto nodded gravely and touched a hand to her cheek. 'And you are the daughter of the *Patrão*, also. It must be hard for a man to approach you.' He frowned suddenly, seizing her left hand. 'I did not ask—I did not think! You have no *noivo*, no lover?'

Charlotte's eyes glittered coldly. 'Do you think for one moment I would have allowed you to make love to me if I had? To be trite, Senhor Monteiro, I'm not that sort of girl.'

'Forgive me.' He raised her hand to his lips, looking up at her in penitence. 'You forget I am a foreigner in your country. You must make allowances for me.'

'Why must I?'

'Because I want you to—very much.' He turned her hand over and pressed a kiss in her palm. 'If I can postpone my flight, will you spend tomorrow with me, Charlotte? Please?'

A few face-saving moments ticked by while Charlotte pretended to give the matter thought, and at last she nodded slowly, rewarded at once by the warmth of his smile.

'You will, *carinha*?' he asked eagerly.

'Yes.' Her teeth caught in her bottom lip. 'I'm not at all sure that I should. Common sense tells me I ought to refuse politely——'

'Common sense!' He caught her to him abruptly. 'If I were wise I know I should go away tomorrow as planned, but I have only to look into your so beautiful face and I am not wise. I want to know you more, to talk to you, learn everything about you.' And he kissed her fiercely and she kissed him back, every part of her fired with response. They were both shaking when she tore herself away at last.

'Roberto, I *must* go. My parents think I'm driving home. They'll worry.'

'*Deus*, of course they will. Forgive me, I am not thinking straight.' He touched her cheek in apology. 'I shall ring for a taxi. Then while we wait for it to arrive we shall drink one last glass of champagne together.'

Charlotte had doubts about the wisdom of more champagne, but before Roberto left the room he resumed his jacket and tie and smiled at her, and reassured she went to the great gilded mirror over the fireplace to tidy her hair. Her eyes shone back at her like stars and she wrinkled her nose at her reflection, then flushed as Roberto's reflection appeared behind her.

'You look even lovelier than before, if that were possible,' said Roberto softly, moving closer. Charlotte gave him an impudent little smile.

'Before what, Senhor Monteiro?'

'Before I did this.' And he turned her in his arms and kissed her again, but gently, with such exquisite tenderness her eyes were brilliant with unshed tears when he raised his head. He touched a fingertip to the corner of one eye, his face troubled. 'Tears, Charlotte? *Não chora, carinha.* Let us drink the champagne, and you will feel better.'

She shook her head. 'Frankly, Roberto, I think I've had more than enough champagne.'

'You mean it was the champagne which moved you to allow my kisses?'

'No. I don't mean that. No amount of alcohol would influence me to allow lovemaking I didn't want. I wanted you to kiss me, Roberto. And you know I did.'

He held her close again. 'Ah, how honest. You are a delight, Charlotte Mercer!'

Charlotte leaned against him, shaken. No one had ever called her a delight before. Mere Latin extravagance, perhaps.

'How early may I telephone you in the morning?' he demanded.

'Whenever you like. William makes sure no one lies in bed in the mornings in the Mercer household.'

Roberto laughed. 'Then as soon as I have contacted the airline I shall ring you, *carinha*. After which I shall come to collect you in your own car, if you permit.'

The doorbell rang. While Roberto went to answer it Charlotte added a touch of lipstick to her mouth, and was putting on her jacket when he returned. She gave him her car keys, and he took them, kissing her fingers.

'I must not disarrange you now you are so dazzlingly perfect once more,' he said.

Charlotte touched a fingertip to his lips, shamelessly pleased when he breathed in sharply in response. 'Thank you for my dinner, Roberto—and for taking the trouble to hand over Mrs Presteigne's gift in person.'

'Trouble?' His smile gleamed white in his dark face. 'If I had known precisely what kind of trouble you would mean, Miss Charlotte Mercer, I think I would have been wise to give the jewels to your parents, as I so much wished to do. Now that I have met you, touched you, kissed you, I fear I shall not sleep tonight—nor for many, many nights to come.'

'Neither shall I!' The words were out before Charlotte could stop them, and she bit her lip, her breath catching as she watched his smile fade and his eyes light with an unmistakable heat.

'Charlotte——' He pulled her towards him but she tugged her hand free.

'The taxi's waiting, Roberto. I must go—it's late.'

He sighed. 'Very well. *Até amanha* then, *querida*. Until tomorrow.'

'Until tomorrow,' she echoed, ignoring a violent urge to beg to stay.

Roberto Monteiro was all formality as he handed Miss Charlotte Mercer into the waiting taxi and expressed very stilted appreciation of the time she had been gracious enough to spare. Charlotte shook his hand and replied in kind, aware of the driver's interest, and kept her eyes rigidly ahead as the taxi moved down the driveway, all the time longing to turn and wave frantically until Roberto was out of sight.

'Well?' demanded her father, the moment she was through the door. He leaned on his stick, barring her way. 'What did Monteiro say, then? Did he accept our offer?'

Charlotte looked utterly blank for a moment, then began to laugh guiltily. 'You're really going to blow your top this time, Dad. I'm afraid I forgot to mention it!'

CHAPTER THREE

'You did what!' Jaker Mercer's roar almost unbalanced him.

'Be careful, Jake,' said his wife. 'Come and sit down. You also, Charlotte.' Janine Mercer examined her daughter's unrepentant face thoughtfully, as she beckoned her to follow them into the sitting-room.

'Keep your hair on, Dad,' said Charlotte, and grinned at her incensed parent. 'Since Roberto's not leaving quite so soon after all, it doesn't really matter. I'll ask him tomorrow; I'm spending the day with him.' Laughter bubbled up inside her at the thunderstruck look on her father's face.

'As I recall, he was most definite about leaving tomorrow, was he not, Jake?' said Janine thoughtfully.

'Aye, he was.' Jake Mercer, his powers of speech restored, looked hard at his glowing daughter. 'Happen he's changed his mind.'

'Happen he has,' mimicked Charlotte.

'Cheeky monkey.' Jake grinned reluctantly. 'I suppose you changed it for him, then.'

'No. He changed it himself. Whereupon I thought it might be more diplomatic to postpone the badgering for a while.' Which was a downright lie. The sale of the Presteigne property had never even crossed Charlotte's mind the entire evening, not that she had the slightest intention of telling her father so. He would think she had gone mad—which wasn't so very far from the truth, if she were honest.

'Where are you going tomorrow, Charlotte?' asked Mrs Mercer.

'No idea, *Maman*. He insisted on sending me home in a taxi tonight, so he's driving the Mini over here in the morning.'

'You like him then, *chérie*?'

'Yes.' Charlotte coloured a little. 'He's charming.'

'I told you he was.' Her mother smiled. 'Now go to bed. You must be tired.'

'And don't come back tomorrow without getting the chap to sell his land to us,' ordered Jake Mercer. 'Mind you, if he's coming round here in the morning there's nothing to stop me asking him myself——'

'No way,' said Charlotte hastily. '*I'll* do it.'

He laughed as she bent to kiss him goodnight. 'All right, lass, I'll leave it to you.'

Charlotte was by no means convinced Jake Mercer would be able to keep his word in this particular instance, so when Roberto Monteiro rang during breakfast she told him she would be waiting at the bottom of the drive when he came, and returned to the breakfast-table with a star-spangled look about her that Janine Mercer viewed with misgiving, since her beloved child had never before displayed such dazed, glittering excitement about any man. While Jake was busy replacing minuscule tyres on one of William's toy cars, she touched Charlotte's hand.

'Take care, *bébé*.'

Charlotte smiled reassuringly. 'Don't worry, *Maman*. Roberto Monteiro is a very civilised man.'

'Aye.' Jake's tone was caustic as he turned back to the table. 'But just remember the "man" bit gets the upper hand over the civilised side most times when a chap's out with a good-looking girl like you.'

'Don't judge everyone by your own standards,' retorted Charlotte, and snatched William up to give him a farewell hug. 'Be good, William Mercer. See you later.'

The little boy's lower lip quivered. 'But it's Saturday today, Charlie. You always stay with me on Saturdays.'

'I will next week,' promised Charlotte, and gave the child to her mother, then swallowed down the rest of her coffee and snatched up her handbag. 'Look at the time. I must fly.'

But as she ran fleetly down the steep bends of the driveway, the thought of the following Saturday struck a chill into her heart. Next Saturday Roberto would be on the other side of the world. Charlotte slowed down to a sedate walk, struck by the thought that last night's mutual enchantment could well have been ephemeral, a thing of the moment and the evening. How would it stand up to the test of the bright light of day, she wondered. But his voice on the phone had been exactly the same, disturbing and vibrant, with the elusive trace of accent that set her pulse racing. She hurried down the last curve to the gates, her heart leaping as she saw her own familiar little car outside, with the tall figure of Roberto Monteiro leaning against it, looking different, younger, in casual white denim trousers and short-sleeved white shirt, a black sweater knotted round his shoulders. He straightened, his eyes lighting up as he saw Charlotte, and for a moment she thought he would catch her in his arms, but he took her hand instead and kissed it.

'*Bom dia*, Charlotte.' He held on to her hand, smiling into her eyes. 'I was so delighted to hear your voice over the telephone I forgot to mention a very important point. I was able to put off my flight for two days, not one. I do not leave until Monday.'

Monday? Charlotte's heart soared. 'Good morning, Roberto,' she said breathlessly. 'You're early.'

He glanced at his watch. 'So are you, Miss Mercer. Could it be that we were both eager to see each other?'

She flushed and tried to withdraw her hand, but he held on to it tightly and she shrugged, laughing. 'Perhaps.'

'You are enchanting,' he said softly. 'Even more beautiful in the sunlight than you were last night. But I so much hoped to see your hair loose.'

'I rarely wear it down.' Charlotte felt bemused, reassured beyond any shadow of a doubt that the magic was still there between them, binding them together as tangibly as a silk cord. 'Shall I drive?' she asked, and he released her hand.

'If you will. Than I shall be free to feast my eyes not only on the beauty of your famous dales, but on you also, *carinha*.' He handed her into the car with care, then slid into the passenger seat with a sigh of pleasure. 'Take me where you will, Charlotte Mercer. I am entirely in your hands.'

Which conjured up such disturbing pictures Charlotte's hands trembled as she started the car. 'Do you fancy wide open spaces, Roberto?'

'*Pois é, senhora*. Of course I do. I am a man of the outdoors, not the city. Also I came prepared. The admirable Millie has packed a picnic basket for us.' Roberto looked so smugly pleased with himself that Charlotte giggled as they left the outskirts of Prestleigh and turned off on a quiet road leading through some of the most picturesque parts of the local countryside, which today had the bonus of warmth and sunlight to put the finishing touch to the perfection of the occasion.

As they explored in leisurely fashion, they talked without stopping, and to Charlotte's joy found a mutual interest in each other's minds as potent as the physical rapport of the evening before. Roberto, however, proved laconic on the subject of his farm in Brazil, brushing it aside in his eagerness to learn everything he could about Charlotte.

'I have cows,' he said, 'and the land where I live is flat—not as pleasing to the eye as these dales of yours.'

'But I thought you had lots of mountains in Brazil,' said Charlotte, surprised.

'We have everything in Brazil, *carinha*. Mountains, jungle, new cities like Brasilia, old colonial towns like Ouro Preto, beaches, rivers——' He shrugged. 'But where I live it is grassland. And cows.'

Charlotte gave her relaxed, handsome passenger a sidelong glance, trying to picture him as a dairy farmer. Her father had some farming friends, but not one of them remotely resembled Roberto Monteiro. She smiled at the thought.

'Why do you smile, Charlotte?' he asked quickly.

'I was trying to picture you in rubber boots, covered in manure, but I failed.'

'For which I am much relieved.' He wrinkled his nose. 'Let us not talk of manure! I wish to talk of you instead.'

Charlotte would have liked to ask him about his family, and most of all about his dead wife, and whether he grieved for her still. Instead she found herself drawn out about a subject never discussed with anyone, of her girlhood dreams of being an artist, of her longing to go to art school, Paris even, to express herself on canvas.

'I thought it wouldn't matter, because I wasn't the son my father wanted.' Charlotte drove slowly between grey stone walls lining a road which wound through sheep-dotted fells. 'Dad thought differently. He decided to make the best of his bargain, and for nineteen years of my life spent a lot of time shaping me into a suitable aspirant to his director's chair. He wouldn't hear of art school. I was sent to business college. And when I qualified I was given a pittance for doing all the odd jobs in the office no one else wanted to do. I'd been at it a year, trying to learn the ropes from the bottom up, when my mother so miraculously presented my father with the son he wanted. So now there's an heir apparent, instead of an heiress, and one of my main functions, as I see it, is to keep William's seat warm.'

Charlotte flipped the indicator and turned down a narrow, stony lane to park the car on a grass verge near a farm gate. 'I know the farmer here quite well,' she told Roberto, smiling. 'He'll recognise the car. So if you can hoist our lunch over that gate, there's a path leading over the fields to a little beck down in a hollow. It's a very effective suntrap on a day like this, and I come here as often as I can in the summer to sunbathe. I keep a rug in the car for the purpose.'

Roberto agreed with alacrity, lifting Charlotte over the gate before following suit with the hamper. 'What is a beck?' he asked, as they started down the path.

'A brook, a little stream down there, hidden by trees and bushes. No one ever seems to come here. Except one or two of your friends now and then.'

'*My* friends?'

'Cows!'

They laughed into each other's eyes and Roberto drew in a deep breath as he lifted his head to the sun. 'I had not thought to be so happy today. And yet I do not feel guilty, because I know Aninha would be glad. I have grieved much for her this past week. I shall miss her, Charlotte. I did not see her very often, but I loved her very much.'

Charlotte squeezed his hand in sympathy. 'I wonder if she's with your grandfather at last. She told me, that last day, that he promised faithfully he'd be waiting for her. I do so hope he was.'

'Their love was very strong.' Roberto helped her over a stile. 'Not everyone experiences such joy in their marriage.'

Had *he*? Charlotte dared not ask, and ran away from him down the slope to the tree-shaded stream, which glittered in the sunlight as it splashed over

the stones and boulders of its bed. Charlotte spread
the wool rug on the grass and made a little curtsy
as Roberto set down the hamper.

'Well?' she demanded. 'Do you approve?'

His eyes lit with a look that set her pulse racing.
'Oh yes. I approve.'

Charlotte dropped to her knees, diving into the
picnic basket to mask her confusion, and Roberto
laughed indulgently and helped her arrange their
lunch on the rug. They sat with their backs to a
mossy bank, eating cold chicken and salad and
wonderful bread baked by Millie. They finished
with wedges of rich fruit cake and crumbly
Wensleydale cheese, and followed it all with the
champagne Roberto had left to chill in the stream
while they ate.

'I shall never drink champagne again without
thinking of you,' said Charlotte pensively.

'While I, Miss Charlotte Mercer, shall need no
reminders.' Roberto's eyes were implicit with memories of the evening before and her colour rose as
he touched a fingertip to her cheek. 'You blush,
carinha. You are thinking the same thoughts as I,
não é?'

Charlotte nodded. It was futile to deny it.
Roberto put her empty glass away in the hamper,
then took her hand, his eyes travelling over her with
proprietorial warmth, from her bare, sandalled feet,
up over her green seersucker dress to her hair,
lingering there for a moment before his free hand
touched the shining red knot. Very gently he began
to remove the pins which held it in place, laying
them in an orderly row on the grass beside him.
The heavy hair tumbled over her shoulders in a

straight, glossy fall, and with a sigh he thrust his hands into it and laid his cheek against it, breathing in its fragrance. He drew back and looked down into her eyes.

'I want to hold you in my arms and kiss you more than anything in the world, Charlotte, but if you say I may not I will lie here and merely look at you, memorise you, just as you are this moment, so that when I am far away I need only close my eyes to see you there in my mind, a portrait of Charlotte no one may share.'

Charlotte was torn. Her body had no doubts. It wanted to push itself close to his, feel his kisses, exult in the strength of his arms. Her brain was more cautious. Another day and Roberto Monteiro would be half-way across the world, leaving Charlotte Mercer to life in Prestleigh, with the like of Alan Bragg and Ben Ackroyd for company. She looked searchingly into the black eyes so close to hers, then yielded herself up to Roberto's arms with a suddenness that took him off balance, and they subsided in a heap together, laughing, the tenseness of the moment gone.

'Shameless,' giggled Charlotte. 'Are you used to women throwing themselves at you?'

'By no means!' He ran his fingers through her hair, lifting the long, burnished strands. 'Ah Charlotte, how grateful I am to Aninha. Do you think she wished us to meet? That this was the reason for asking me to give you the pearls personally—why, what is it, *carinha*?'

She gazed at him in remorse. 'Roberto—I forgot all about the pearls! I put them safe in my bag on the way home and never gave them another thought. They're still there in my room.' Her teeth sank into her lower lip.

Roberto reached out a finger and touched her lip. 'Do not, *carinha*. You will hurt your mouth. What made you forget the pearls?'

'Not what. Who!' Charlotte smiled slowly and he caught his breath and closed his eyes, clenching his teeth. She touched his lip in turn. 'Please kiss me, Roberto—if you want.'

'Oh, I want!' he said fiercely, his lids flying open to disclose a look of such heat that she shivered and melted against him, seeking his mouth blindly as his arms tightened round her. The sun filtered down through the leaves of the trees, dappling the grass with shifting patterns of light. The beck splashed on merrily, the only sound in the hidden hollow as the figures on the rug lay locked in motionless embrace for long, breathless minutes, until Roberto raised his head at last to look down at Charlotte's dazed face.

Gently, reverently almost, he touched a hand to her cheek, brushing away a lock of hair before tracing a path down her throat, his fingers halting at the low neckline of her dress. Charlotte lay quiescent, not even caring that she was behaving recklessly because, in spite of the heat raging in both of them, she felt nothing but trust in the man holding her so close to his hard, muscular body that she was left in doubt as to how much he wanted her.

'Charlotte,' he said huskily. 'I long to touch, to caress, but I fear to offend you. Tell me we must leave this enchanted place and I shall obey at once—even though I want so much to stay.'

'Then stay,' she said, and turned her face up to his, filled with a surge of elation as he tensed and gasped when her fingers slid beneath his shirt to stroke the broad chest beneath. He gave a stifled groan and sought the buttons of her dress, pulling them open in desperate haste so that his fingers could caress her breasts through the lace that covered them. Then even that slight barrier was too much and he dispensed with it summarily, bending his head to kiss the taut globes laid bare to his eyes and hands.

Charlotte gave a stifled cry, and he returned his mouth to hers, one arm tightening about her waist while his other hand stroked and teased her breasts until she was at fever-pitch with longing.

'Roberto——' she gasped, and he crushed her against him with both arms, her breasts against his bare chest as he rubbed his cheek against her hair, murmuring broken endearments in Portuguese. He raised his head at last and stared down at her, his face stern with the desire he was holding in check.

'I want you, *querida*. Do you want *me*?'

Charlotte went very still, then drew away and began to do up her dress. 'I want you more than I realised was possible. But I can't let you make love to me.'

Roberto turned over on his stomach and lay face down. 'I know it,' he said indistinctly after a lengthy interval. 'I have known from the start that I could not have you, Charlotte, even though one look at you was enough to tell me how it would be between us.'

Charlotte was dangerously close to tears as she pinned up her hair, lingering over it to give herself time to recover. 'You go away on Monday,' she said quietly. 'Perhaps I'll never see you again. And in Prestleigh it would hardly do for Jake Mercer's daughter to produce a fatherless brat.'

Roberto sat up, his eyes appalled. '*Meu deus*, Charlotte——'

She shook her head at him ruefully. 'You commented on my honesty last night. I've enough of my father in me to come to the point. And the point is, Roberto Monteiro, that I don't sleep around. In fact, if you had—had proceeded further just now you would have succeeded in doing more than any other man has ever done.'

His eyes lit with a possessive gleam. 'You are a virgin, *querida*?'

'Emotive word, isn't it?' She got up, smoothing down her skirt. 'Rather a joke, I suppose, in this day and age. Nevertheless, it's the truth. But believe me, Roberto, I wanted badly to give you the—the——'

'Unique privilege of such a gift?' He came to his feet, taking her by the shoulders. 'I must leave on Monday, Charlotte. I am needed at home. But I will return. You have my word. Word of a Monteiro.' He looked down at her searchingly. 'But the time before I leave I beg you will spend with me. I promise on my grandmother's grave I shall not try again to seduce you.'

'The problem is, you don't really have to try,' said Charlotte bluntly, and colour rose darkly in his lean cheeks.

'*Amada*, if you have any feelings for me at all do not say things like that!'

'I'll try to be more devious,' she promised solemnly, and bent to pick up the rug, flushing bright red as she discovered her bra lying abandoned on the grass. 'Oh dear! Turn your back while I put it on. I don't relish facing *Maman* without it.'

He gave a choked laugh and turned away, folding the rug while Charlotte remedied the deficit, and on the way home followed her lead in keeping the conversation as neutral as possible. When they reached Prestleigh Charlotte skirted the town to make for Presteigne House, and as they drew up on the terrace Roberto turned to her urgently.

'Will you dine here again with me tonight, Charlotte?'

She looked at him doubtfully. 'I don't think that's wise——'

'I have given my word.' His chin lifted. 'I do not break promises.'

'Oh I'm not doubting *you*, Roberto.' Her eyes danced. 'It's myself I'm worrying about.'

His answering smile was tender. 'Ah, *carinha*, if I had...'

'World enough and time?'

'Como?'

'I was quoting Marvell, a seventeenth-century English poet. He was coaxing a coy mistress to his bed in verse. He'd have sympathy with you, wouldn't he?' Her eyes teased him, and he caught her hand and kissed it.

'Say you will come to me, Charlotte. I would take you out to dine, but——' he shrugged expressively.

'But my red head is too well known, and you are so exotically *un*known, all the right conclusions would be drawn.' Charlotte gave in, as she had known she would from the first. 'All right. Since you've postponed your flight, the least I can do is keep you comapany.'

For a moment Roberto Monteiro showed every sign of seizing his companion in his arms, but after a brief fight with himself he leapt out of the car, bending to look at Charlotte through the open window. '*Muito obrigado,* Miss Charlotte Mercer. Thank you for taking pity on my loneliness. *Até ja*. Which means "see you later". But not too much later,' he added, and smiled.

CHAPTER FOUR

IT TOOK a lot of fast talking to convince Jake Mercer that the right opportunity had still not presented itself to discuss the sale of Roberto Monteiro's land. Charlotte produced the pearl necklace and earrings by way of distraction, which slowed her father up a little, though Janine Mercer quite evidently found it hard to understand how Charlotte could have simply forgotten to hand over the earrings the moment she got home from Presteigne House the night before.

'This Roberto Monteiro must be quite a man,' she said, shaking her head.

'Aye.' Jake peered at his daughter suspiciously. 'I don't know that I'm easy about all this, Charlotte. D'you mean to say you're off to Presteigne House again tonight! Why the devil didn't you ask the chap to eat with us here?'

'And have you throwing out sledge-hammer hints about golf courses all night!' Charlotte shook her head. 'Not on your life. But I promise I'll make my bid at the opportune moment. I've got until tomorrow night.'

'Tomorrow night!' Jake exchanged looks with his wife. 'Now look here, Charlotte, I don't want you losing your head over this chap. You'll probably never see him again.'

Janine put a restraining hand on his. 'Do not distress yourself, *chéri*, our daughter is no fool.'

Her eyes met Charlotte's. 'Remember we trust you. Always.'

Charlotte shook her head in wonder. 'I'm a big girl, you know! I won't let him have his evil way with me, which I assume is what all these parental jitters are about.'

'No,' said her mother, before Jake could explode in protest. 'It is not your physical wellbeing that concerns me, *bébé*. I do not wish you to be unhappy. Afterwards.'

'Your parents do not object to your dining alone here with me a second time, Charlotte?' asked Roberto, when they were alone together after another of Millie Sutton's splendid meals.

'They have reservations,' she admitted.

'Tomorrow I shall present myself to them and reassure your parents that I intend no harm to their daughter.'

'No!' said Charlotte instantly. 'I mean, I'd rather spend the time alone with you, Roberto, please. If you want that, of course.'

He slid an arm behind her and drew her close. 'How could you doubt it, *chica*? Shall we drive again tomorrow? Though perhaps this time we might find somewhere less—less private for our lunch, yes? I do not think my resolutions would survive another champagne picnic in the sun alone with you.' He raised her face to his. 'I gave you a promise that will be hard to keep—but I *shall* keep it, *com certeza*.'

And he did. The rest of the evening passed in watching television, listening to music, and just talking, since Roberto seemed determined to learn every last thing about Charlotte she was willing to tell. And next day, despite protests from her parents, she went driving with Roberto again. They ate their lunch at a country pub, and walked a short way afterwards over the moors, where the peace and isolation seemed to make it possible for Roberto to talk at length about his childhood and the early loss of his mother, of the father who had brought him up to the traditional life of the pampas.

They leaned against a farm gate together as Roberto finally made a brief mention of his marriage to Amalha Braga when he was little more than twenty years old. 'I was, I think you say, wet still behind the ears.'

'What happened to Amalha, Roberto?' Charlotte asked.

'She had an accident, while out riding alone. Her horse threw her. Her neck was broken. She died all alone out there in the *campo*, with only the grass and sky for company.'

'Oh God, Roberto, how tragic!' Charlotte hugged him close, burrowing her face against his chest, aching with sympathy for him. His arms tightened around her and they stood together in silent communion until a sudden shower of rain sent them running for the car. And this time Roberto persuaded Charlotte to stay at Presteigne House until the evening, with no detour home to bathe and change before dinner.

'Let us not waste the time,' he said as they went into the house. 'You are beautiful as you are. Please ring your mother and say the so selfish Roberto Monteiro wishes to monopolise her daughter even more.'

Charlotte was only too willing to agree, and revelled later in the domesticity of serving him the cold dinner Millie Sutton had left for them before she went off to church.

'How I wish I did not have to leave in the morning.' Roberto looked across the dining-table at her with sombre eyes. 'I would like to call on your parents, meet this so lovable little brother of yours, behave as a man should under these circumstances.'

'There's no time for that,' said Charlotte flatly. 'I'd rather you concentrated on me than my family since you're off so soon.' She sighed. 'But I'm going to miss you. Do you know, Senhor Monteiro, that after a mere day or two of your acquaintance life is going to seem a very flat business without you when you're gone.'

His eyes kindled. 'I promise I shall return as soon as I can.'

'And you never break a promise!'

'Never.' He raised his glass to her and they toasted each other silently, then Roberto rose to his feet, holding out his hand. 'Come, Charlotte. Let us go back to Aninha's drawing-room and sit together and pretend tomorrow is a million years away.'

Neither of them wanted music tonight, or television, or anything other than to hold each other close, in mutual comfort against the parting looming over them.

'I wish there were something I could do to preserve this moment.' said Charlotte huskily. 'Capture it somehow and keep it for when you're thousands of miles away on your farm.'

'I too, *querida*.' His voice roughened. 'In such a short time you have become so necessary to me I dread the prospect of leaving you behind.' He raised her face to his suddenly, his eyes blazing into hers. 'Come with me, Charlotte! Come home with me to Rio Grande do Sul.'

She stared at him, shaken. 'Oh Roberto, I wish I could, but I can't just run away from everything at the drop of a hat. Besides, it's too soon, too sudden.'

'You mean you do not wish to come with me?' he said harshly, his face darkening.

'No! I do, I do! But I have a responsible job. I can't just walk out of it. Particularly now my father's out of action.' Charlotte breathed in deeply, mention of her father reminding her that time was running out, that she still hadn't broached the subject of the Presteigne estate. She looked away, feeling wretched. 'And there's something else, Roberto.' She felt him stiffen.

'Something else? Tell me!' he commanded.

'I have something to ask you. I should have brought it up before, but somehow the time never seemed right.'

The urgency faded slowly from his face. He looked at her searchingly, then moved away, releasing her. He leaned back against the buttoned velvet sofa-back, arms folded, watching Charlotte closely. 'If I can be of assistance to you in any way, Charlotte,' he said with formality, 'I am, of course, yours to command.'

Charlotte sat bold upright at the other end of the sofa, staring down at her clasped hands, wishing now she had let her father do his own dealing after all. 'Roberto,' she began with reluctance, 'on behalf of the Mercer Group I've been instructed to ask you if you will sell your land.'

Roberto stared at her, dumbfounded. '*Minha terra*—my land?'

'Yes.' She turned to him. 'The Presteigne estate is yours now. For years my father tried to persuade your grandmother to sell the land to him, and now you've inherited he's making the request to you.' Charlotte watched with foreboding as the warmth and animation drained from his face.

'I see,' he said after a while.

She put out her hands in appeal. 'We're offering a very fair price——'

'You mean you are not presuming on the—acquaintance between you and me to secure a *pechincha*—a bargain!' His eyes held a chill gleam of mockery.

Charlotte went on doggedly. 'My father thought you might have no use for the land since you farm in Brazil. In his experience farmers usually need money, and he hoped you might be no exception.'

'So Mr Jacob Mercer sent his beautiful daughter to—to persuade me.' Roberto's tone cut Charlotte to the heart.

'It wasn't like that at all,' she cried desperately. 'He was anxious to ask you for an appointment for himself on the day of the funeral, but before he had the chance you asked to see me instead. So he left it to me to bring up the subject of the sale.'

'It has taken you a long time to do so.' His smile was sardonic. 'Why then did you not make your offer that first night?'

Charlotte's eyes fell. 'I think you know why.'

'Oh, yes. I believe I do! When you discovered I was ready to put off my return to Brazil solely to see more of you I think you decided to exploit my feelings to the full.' Roberto got to his feet and lit a cigar, then strolled over to the marble fireplace. He turned to face his unhappy guest, standing with legs planted astride as he scrutinised her coldly through the curling blue smoke. 'And what does your father want with this land? Is it for a factory, or a nuclear power station?' He gestured towards the window. 'Or perhaps he has received inside knowledge of some proposed motorway in the vicinity, so that he may reap the reward by reselling my family's land at a profit.'

'That's not true—or fair.' Charlotte's eyes flashed at him stormily. 'You're angry with me, which I suppose I expected, but I can't allow you to slander my father. He's a businessman, not a crook. His only aim is to create a golf course and country club here, a place where the people of Prestleigh can come to keep fit and relax. No matter. I'll tell him he can forget it.' She rose to her feet, looking about her for her sweater. 'I'd better go.'

Roberto's eyes glittered suddenly, and he threw his cigar into the fireplace. He walked towards her with his graceful swagger, looking foreign and alien to her, a very different man from her companion of the past day or two. 'I'm disappointed, Charlotte. Surely you are going to continue with your so successful campaign of seducing me into giving you what you want?'

Charlotte backed away, deeply disturbed by the aura of menace exuding from him. 'It's what my father wants, not me. And I've never tried to seduce you—or anyone else.'

'No?' He smiled slowly. 'Then what have you been doing ever since we met, *querida*, if not trying to persuade me in a way you were sure I would find irresistible?'

Her chin lifted. 'What happened between us happened naturally. I didn't ask you the first night for the simple reason that I forgot. Silly, isn't it? I'm usually hyper-efficient over business matters. Then I didn't ask you yesterday because I couldn't bring myself to spoil our day together. I only brought the subject up now because I couldn't go home to my father a third time and say I hadn't mentioned it before you left. So there it is. I'll report that your answer's negative.'

'Are you not going to bribe me, Charlotte?' He moved swiftly, and caught her by the elbows, his eyes burning into hers. 'Is there no gift you can offer me, poor farmer that I am, that will tempt me to give you what you want?'

Suspicion flowered in Charlotte's mind, bleaching the colour from her tanned face. 'What exactly are you saying?'

His smile was wolfish. 'There is something in your possession any man would covet, is there not?' And he reached behind her and pulled away the scarf that tied her hair at the nape of her neck. The heavy red hair swung forward, one strand coming down over her face, and Roberto swept it aside, thrusting his hands into the the shining mass to hold her head still as his eyes locked with hers. 'Well, Charlotte? What do you say? A house and two hundred acres at whatever price your father is offering, but with one small added—how do you say? Incentive?'

Charlotte glared at him. 'I don't know what you mean.'

'Ah yes you do, *querida*.' He smiled with cold brilliance. 'Your father may have what he wishes, if I also may gain the desire of my heart—and my body.'

'Both my father and I would consider the price too high,' retorted Charlotte with disdain. 'I'm afraid my—my virginity isn't up for grabs, Senhor Monteiro. No sale. You can keep your precious acres.' She tore herself out his grasp and ran for the door, but he was there before her, his back thrust against it.

'I want you, Charlotte,' he said harshly, 'and I mean to have you. Now! Whether you wish it or not...'

Suddenly there were voices outside in the hall and a knock at the door, and with a savage curse Roberto moved away to let in Millie Sutton.

'Just to let you know I'm back, Roberto,' said the housekeeper, her cheerful smile fading as looked from one strained face to the other. 'I thought the pair of you might like some coffee and a slice or two of the cake I baked this afternoon.'

Charlotte smiled at her with passionate gratitude. 'You're so kind, Mrs Sutton, but I was just leaving.' She brushed past Roberto, and followed the housekeeper into the hall. 'Goodbye,' she said to him, avoiding his eyes. 'Safe journey. Goodnight, Mrs Sutton, thank you for the delicious supper.'

'Charlotte——' Robert strode after her as she hurried out to her car, but she dived inside, on fire to get away. He wrenched open the passenger door urgently.

'Charlotte—*listen, por favor.*'

'*Listen?*' she spat. 'As far as I'm concerned, Roberto Monteiro, you've already said more than enough. Get out of my way. I'm going home.'

'Go then,' he grated, and slammed the door shut and Charlotte spun the car on the terrace and shot off in a spurt of gravel, desperate to get away from Presteigne House and its new owner as fast as was humanly possible.

CHAPTER FIVE

THE Mercer household was a fraught place for a long time after Charlotte's return to the fold that fateful Sunday evening. For once Jake Mercer found he was obliged to tread very warily in his daughter's vicinity instead of the other way round, and Janine Mercer's heart was heavy as she tried to do everything in her power to make life more bearable for her aloof, withdrawn daughter.

'Sorry,' Charlotte said tersely, that first night. 'I'm afraid I made a mess of it, Dad. No deal.'

'He wouldn't sell?' asked Jake with commendable calm, sensitive for once to the bleak misery in his daughter's beautiful eyes.

'Shall we say the price was a bit high?'

'You could have given way a bit.'

'Not as much as Senhor Monteiro wanted.' Charlotte smiled wearily. 'Pity you didn't do the dealing yourself after all, Dad. I'll be glad when you're back in the driving-seat again.'

The admission worried her mother deeply, since no one knew better than Mrs Mercer how much Charlotte had enjoyed her brief time of freedom at the Mercer Group, in spite of the added work-load.

'Well, don't fret about it, love,' said Jake, unusually magnanimous. 'It's only a few acres of dirt, after all. Not worth losing any sleep over.'

Charlotte agreed in principle, but lost the sleep just the same. If this was love, and presumably it was, she thought in misery, she would take good care never to leave herself open to it again. Not that she was ever again likely to meet anyone even remotely like Roberto Gaspar Monteiro. One of a kind, she thought bitterly, and wept scalding tears into her pillow night after night.

Charlotte was more glad of her job in the days that followed than she had ever been before. She started work early and finished late, and occupied her evenings and weekends with William, Alan Bragg, and sometimes, in desperation, even Ben Ackroyd. Anything was better than brooding over Roberto Monteiro and the damage he had done. And when, eventually, Jake Mercer returned to his desk life took on a semblance of normality, until a day a little over a month after the fateful weekend with Roberto Monteiro, when an airmail letter arrived for Jake Mercer in his capacity of Managing Director of the Mercer Group. Charlotte opened it, as usual, with rest of the mail, then dropped the thin sheet of paper as if it had burned her fingers.

'You'd better take a look at this, Dad,' she said, taking it into him with the rest of the mail.

'Eh?' he said absently, deep in one of Ben Ackroyd's reports. 'What is it?'

'A letter from Roberto Monteiro.'

'Is it, by God?' Jake snatched up the letter and scanned it eagerly, his eyebrows shooting to his fiery thatch of his hair. 'You've read this, Charlotte?'

'I have indeed. Interesting, isn't it?'

'You don't have to do it,' he said flatly.

'You want the Presteigne estate, don't you?'

'You know damn well I do. But not if it means any harm to you.'

Charlotte sat down on the chair in front of the desk and examined her nails. 'He makes a lot of conditions.'

'He does that! Not backward about it, is he?'

'He knows you want the place. And he's prepared to agree to a reasonable price as long as you buy Presteigne House with the land and use it as the clubhouse, employ Millie Sutton in some capacity if she wishes it, and name the place the Presteigne Golf and Country Club.'

'Only the whole shebang seems to depend on Miss Charlotte Mercer travelling out to Brazil with the contract on behalf of the Mercer Group.' Jake Mercer snorted and returned to the formally phrased letter in front of him. 'The chap "understands" that my injury makes it inconvenient for me to travel myself, and, since it is impossible for him to return to this country in the near future, he would be obliged if Miss Mercer spared the time to fly to Porto Alegre, expenses paid.' He looked up. 'Reading between the lines, I take it that means you go or I can whistle for the land.'

'I'll go,' said Charlotte.

'You don't have to!'

'Oh, but I do.' She smiled in a way that made her father shift in his chair uneasily. 'I've got some unfinished business with Roberto Monteiro, Dad, as it happens. I won't be easy in my mind until I've rounded it off to my own satisfaction.'

Mrs Mercer was appalled when she heard the news that evening. 'You are not serious in this, Charlotte? You cannot mean to travel all that way to meet this young man alone!'

'That's all I'm going to do—meet him. I shan't stay with him. I'll book a room in Porto Alegre, which seems to be the main city in his area. He can just get himself there to sign the contract, since it's obvious he needs the money pretty badly after all.' Charlotte's face was coldly determined.

'Now look, lass,' began Jake uneasily, 'I think this has gone far enough. I'll find other land for my golf club.'

'No, Dad. I'm going. It's something I just have to do.'

Janine Mercer eyed her daughter's stony face with disapproval. 'Me, I say you should not go alone.'

'I'll be very careful, I promise, *Maman*.' Charlotte turned to her father. 'Only I'd rather you paid my fare and the hotel. I don't want to be beholden to—to him for anything.'

The Mercers were deeply perturbed at the idea of their beautiful daughter travelling on her own to Brazil, however much she was bent on it, though Jake's resolve had a tendency to waver slightly at the prospect of gaining his heart's desire. Not that it mattered. Charlotte's mind was made up. Nothing was going to deprive her of the golden opportunity of throwing money in person in Roberto Monteiro's handsome face. Even so, she refused to hurry off to Porto Alegre the following week, as Roberto had suggested with frigid courtesy in his letter. It was a full six weeks before Miss Charlotte Mercer could spare the time to travel to Rio Grande do Sul, she wrote in reply, and spent the time in trying to learn a few useful phrases of Portuguese, and constructing a protective shell over the hurt suffered at Roberto Monteiro's hands.

'*Chérie,* I do not like to see you go,' said Mrs Mercer, as she bade her daughter a reluctant goodbye at Heathrow Airport. 'I implore you to be careful. Do nothing foolish, *bébé.*'

Charlotte embraced her mother lovingly. 'I'll be just fine. I know exactly what I'm doing.'

'That,' said Janine drily, 'is what troubles me, *chérie.*'

'You be a sensible lass as usual,' commanded her father. 'Don't go out alone at night, and come straight back the minute you've got Monteiro's signature on the dotted line.'

'I don't know how long that will take, remember,' Charlotte warned. 'But I'll be back as soon as I can. Give William a kiss for me. Tell him I'll bring him back a great big present.'

'Never mind the presents—just get yourself back here safe and sound,' said Jake gruffly, as his wife gave Charlotte a final hug.

In actual fact Charlotte was happier than she had been for some time as she boarded the aeroplane bound for Rio de Janeiro. She was no stranger to air travel and loved the excitement and bustle of it all, the comfort of the first-class section of the plane, even the food, which was very good. But she firmly refused the champagne offered her, unable to bear the taste of it since her experience with Roberto Monteiro. For the first time in weeks she allowed herself to think about him at length during the flight, wondering, as she had so often before, what would have happened that last night if Millie Sutton's arrival had been even half an hour later.

Her lips tightened. She would never, ever, allow herself to get into a similar situation again, not with Roberto Monteiro or any other man. It was galling to think she had only herself to blame. If she were stupid enough to make a practice of announcing her virgin state to the world it was only to be expected that some man or other would see it as a challenge and try to take it away from her, if only for the novelty of the experience.

When she reached Rio de Janeiro Charlotte found she had no time to explore the fabled beauty of the city, since her connecting flight to Porto Alegre left only a couple of hours later. She spent the time in freshening herself up and changing her clothes, then had a snack before she boarded the plane on the next stage of her journey. Her meagre stock of newly acquired Portuguese phrases came in very useful, but Charlotte quickly found it was much easier to phrase her own careful words than to understand the flood of voluble response she received every time in answer, and reverted to English during the flight, since it was spoken by all the aircrew on board.

Porto Alegre proved to be a fast-growing port which gave an immediate impression of prosperity. Since there was no rush to reach the hotel, Charlotte asked the taxi-driver to take her on a small tour of the city en route, and was given quick glimpses of the old residential part of the city on the high ground dominated by the Governor's Palace before being whisked past an imposing cathedral and the twin white towers of an old church with a name the taxi-driver translated as Our Lady of Pain. She grew quite dizzy as the cab hurtled along streets which wound in and around and up and down, until Charlotte was glad to get a brief look at the huge, green-grassed park of Farroupilha, which she was told was the site of a zoo and botanical gardens, and on weekends and holidays served as a setting for folk-dancing. Situated at the junction of five rivers, Porto Alegre could hardly fail to be busy, she thought, as the taxi finally took her at hair-raising speed to the hotel she had chosen, the Plaza São Rafael, which was large and luxurious enough to satisfy her father and mother, and central enough to make it ideal for her stay. Tomorrow, she thought with satisfaction, Roberto Monteiro would be here in person, as she had stipulated, and she would throw down contract and cheque in front of him in one of the public rooms, after which she would be free to go home again with a quiet mind, all the ends tidied up and the gaping wound left by his eruption into her life soothed by her pleasure in handing him the money he hadn't been able to resist after all.

When Charlotte was shown to her luxuriously furnished room at the Plaza São Rafael, she flopped down on one of the twin beds and rang her parents to say she had arrived safely, then ordered a meal from room-service for later in the evening before taking a much needed nap. She slept like the dead until the waiter arrived with the crayfish salad she had ordered, and Charlotte tipped the man reck-lessly and fell to on her meal with relish. After-wards she took a long, leisurely bath, dwelling with pleasure on the interview with Roberto in the morning, and decided to go straight back to bed to prepare for it. Suddenly her body seemed to be demanding all the sleep it had missed out on for the past weeks, and she smiled sleepily at the thought that only a day or two of Roberto Monteiro's acquaintance had resulted in two months or more of insomnia. Now all that was at an end. No more nonsense of that sort. She would soon be able to settle his hash once and for all.

Charlotte woke early next morning, feeling refreshed, with no traces of jet-lag, and enjoyed the rolls and orange juice and wonderful black coffee brought to her. Afterwards she took a shower and spent some time in coiling her hair severely on top of her head, then dressed in her black linen suit with a severe white silk shirt. She was putting the careful finishing touches to her face when the telephone rang and one of the hotel receptionists informed her a man wished to speak with her and would await her in the foyer. Charlotte's heart missed a beat.

'Did he give a name?' she asked.

'*Não, senhora*. He has a letter for you.'

A letter? Charlotte scowled at the receiver, then took the lift down to the foyer, where one of the receptionists pointed to a man Charlotte had never seen before. Her heart nose-dived. So Roberto hadn't deigned to come in person after all. Did he honestly have the effrontery to think she would deal with him through a third person after travelling thousands of miles just to see him? To sign the contract, she corrected herself hurriedly, and went towards the man, who was weather-beaten, with an Indian cast of features, and looked as though the rather wrinkled suit he wore was not his customary garb.

'*Bom dia*. Charlotte Mercer,' she said to him crisply.

The man bowed courteously. '*Muito prazer, senhora. Seja bemvindo.*'

'I'm afraid I speak very little Portuguese,' she said and the man nodded gravely.

'I am Jorge Pires, *senhora*. I have a letter from Senhor Monteiro.' He held out an envelope and Charlotte took it with a brief word of thanks.

'An emergency at the farm prevents me from travelling to meet you,' wrote Roberto. 'I would be obliged if you would accompany Jorges Pires, who is an entirely trustworthy companion, on the journey I beg you will take. A bereavement makes it impossible for me to keep our original appointment, but my employer has consented to allow you private accommodation here at Estancia Velha. If you prefer, you need see no more of me than is necessary for the signing of the contract for the Presteigne Estate. You will be escorted back to Porto Alegre as soon as you wish. I apologise for the need to inconvenience you in this way.'
                          Roberto Monteiro.

Charlotte's jaw clenched. She glanced at the weathered face watching her. 'Senhor Pires. When must I leave for——' She looked back at the note. 'Estancia Velha. Is it far?'

'An hour away, *senhora*.'

Charlotte made up her mind quickly. She had a rapid consultation with the receptionist who spoke the most fluent American English, secured her room for a week, then went up to pack her belongings.

Jorge Pires had a taxi waiting when Charlotte returned to the foyer.

'How do we get to Estancia Velha, Senhor Pires?' she asked as they set off through the bustling city.

'We fly, *senhora*,' was the laconic reply. And fly they did, in a small, light aircraft, to Charlotte's surprise, with Jorge Pires himself at the controls. She barely had time to voice her astonishment before her companion received radio permission to take off and they were airborne. When the required altitude had been reached, the Brazilian smiled at her in kind reassurance

'Do not be nervous, *senhora*.'

'I'm not,' she assured him, eyes sparkling. 'I'm exhilarated—this is wonderful! Whose plane is it?'

The man's smile was indulgent as his passenger looked down in excitement as they passed lush soybean fields, and green plateaux which stretched into the blue haze of the distance.

'It is the property of the *Patrão*, senhora.'

Charlotte looked up at him quickly. 'Does Senhor Monteiro work for this *Patrão* of yours?'

'*Sim, senhora.*'

Charlotte longed to question him further, but as he was obviously not disposed to talk further she left Jorge Pires to his controls and concentrated on the view below. Soon all she could see was a rolling ocean of green, topped in places by great patches of brown, and she had time to wonder about the 'private accommodation' Roberto mentioned in his letter. His employer was very kind to offer to put her up, she admitted, trying to be fair, but all this

was a far cry from the civilised, public encounter
all worked out so neatly to take place in the hotel
in Porto Alegre.

'Is Estancia Velha far from the airport, Senhor
Pires?' she asked after a while.

He shook his head. 'No airport, *senhora*.
Estancia Velha has a private landing strip.'

Charlotte's eyes widened. 'Really!'

'Senhor Monteiro will be waiting when we land.'

He'd better be, thought Charlotte fiercely, and
set herself to wait in patience for their arrival, which
was sooner than expected. Almost at once she
caught sight of a group of tall trees clustering
around a large white house, with other buildings
grouped behind it. Her pilot began the descent with
the calm expertise of long practice and brought the
plane in to land some distance away from the house
and buildings, touching down at last well out of
sight on a short landing-strip of packed red earth
cut through the green grass to point like an arrow
at a small building Charlotte assumed must be the
hangar for the aircraft.

She felt an involuntary tightening in her stomach
as nerves and excitement and a sudden unbidden
rush of anticipation all combined to make her heart
beat faster at the prospect of meeting Roberto
Gaspar Monteiro again. But as the red landing-strip
rushed up to meet them Charlotte frowned. There
seemed to be no one in sight.

As the small plane taxied to a halt Jorge Pires
gestured to a cloud of dust in the distance. 'He
comes,' he said briefly, and jumped to the ground,
then came round to help Charlotte alight.

She heard a thunder of hooves as the cloud of dust resolved itself into a group of horsemen who reined in to a sudden, theatrical standstill only a few feet away from the spot where Charlotte stood riveted, eyes frankly goggling at the man who spurred his horse a slight distance apart from the rest and sat easily in the saddle, his eyes grave and unsmiling as he inclined his head in greeting. Roberto Monteiro, like all the men behind him, wore a flat, chinstrap hat, a neckerchief tied at the open collar of his shirt, balloon-pleated breeches, and loose, creased leather boots with spurs. A hide belt adorned with silver medallions encircled his spare waist, a revolver in a holster hung at one side, a string of wooden beads and a gleaming, silver-sheathed knife at the other.

'Welcome, Miss Mercer,' said this exotic, unfamiliar personage, and removed his hat with ceremony.

Charlotte stared at him, lost for words. So much for green wellies and manure! She found her voice with an effort, wondering if this was all a dream, or if she had wandered by mistake on to some film set. 'Good morning, Senhor Monteiro.'

Roberto waved a hand at the group behind him. 'The men who work with me,' he said briefly, and turned to them with a rattle of Portuguese Charlotte interpreted as her introduction to the group of dark-skinned men, who smiled at her and touched their hatbrims. She smiled back rather shyly, as Roberto swung himself from his horse and handed the reins to Jorge Pires.

'Come,' Roberto said to Charlotte. 'I shall drive you to the house.' He picked up Charlotte's suitcase and strode off to a jeep parked alongside the hangar, and she hurried after the jangling, spurred figure of her not very welcoming host. The others departed immediately, Charlotte stumbling a little as she looked over her shoulder in wonder at the superb display of horsemanship as they rode off at breakneck speed.

'Where are they going?' she asked breathlessly, as she tried not to display too much leg as she negotiated the step of the jeep.

'To rejoin the herd.' Roberto backed out the jeep and to her surprise drove off in the opposite direction from the group of main buildings Charlotte had seen as she flew in.

'Where am I to stay?' she asked, holding on to her seat for dear life as the jeep bucketed its way along a track through the unending grassland.

'At my house.' Roberto stared straight ahead, ignoring the incensed look Charlotte shot at him.

'*Your* house!'

'Do not disturb yourself. I shall sleep with the other men while you are here.'

'Oh. This place you're taking me to—is it your farm?'

'No. It is my house.'

Charlotte gave up. Roberto Monteiro was plainly not in the mood for talk, and she was most certainly not in the mood to persuade him. It seemed a long time before she sighted a small house in the distance. It looked rather like a miniature of the one seen from the plane. A cluster of trees protected it, but there was no garden as such, only a patch of clipped turf outside and a vine-covered stable and outhouses near by. Roberto drew up near the shallow steps of the veranda fronting the small, compact little building, which had newly whitened walls and a roof of curving rust-red tiles supported by two vine-clad pillars.

'*Bemvindo*, Charlotte,' he said formally, as he handed her down from the jeep. 'Welcome to my house.'

Charlotte eyed him doubtfully. 'Since it's such a short airflight from Porto Alegre is it really necessary for me to stay here at all?'

'Jorge Pires had other duties. He is needed elsewhere and cannot fly you back to Porto Alegre today.' Roberto took her suitcase and went into the house, motioning Charlotte to follow him. She shrugged and crossed the veranda to enter a room with simple chintz-covered furniture and dark carved chairs flanking a small dining-table.

'*A sala de estar e jantar,*' Roberto announced. 'Both living-room and dining-room.'

Charlotte made no comment and followed him into a narrow hall leading to a bedroom, a bathroom and a small kitchen, every room newly painted and neat, but surprisingly bare. As they reached the kitchen a young girl in a print dress came in from outside and smiled shyly at Charlotte.

'This is Teresa,' said Roberto. 'She is your maid, also your——' he frowned, searching for the word.

'Chaperon?' suggested Charlotte sweetly.

He shrugged. 'If you like.' He turned to the girl. '*Teresa, Dona Carlota deve ser cansada. A cama e pronta?*'

'*E, sim, senhor.*'

'*Bom. Tem café?*'

'*Tenho. Vou trazer n'a varanda agora mesmo.*'

Charlotte's studies of the Portuguese language almost prompted her to say she wasn't at all tired, and certainly didn't want to go to bed, but it hardly seemed worth arguing, and the prospect of coffee, at least, was welcome and familiar in this new, enormous land.

'Where are your cows?' asked Charlotte, as she took the rattan chair he drew out for her on the veranda. Roberto looked surprised. He tossed aside his hat and leaned against one of the stone pillars as he lit a cigar.

'Did you not see them as you flew in?'

'No——' Charlotte halted, staring at him incredulously. 'I saw great brown patches on the grassland. Do you mean *they* were all cows?'

He smiled faintly, and for a moment looked more like the man she had lost her heart to, but the warmth was only fleeting, and Charlotte turned away at once as the pretty, dark-skinned Teresa came out of the house with the promised coffee.

'Muita obrigada,' she said with deliberate care, and the girl smiled, delighted.

'De nada, Dona Carlota,' she said happily and took herself off.

'You have been learning Portuguese?' asked Roberto, looking amused.

'Just a few words to help me get by on the journey. ''Dona Carlota'' sounds very grand, by the way,' she added, as she filled their cups with strong fragrant coffee. 'Do you take it black?' she asked pointedly, though she remembered only too well how he liked his coffee, and everything else about him, too, to her regret.

'Thank you, yes.'

'Do all the cattle I saw belong to the man you work for?' asked Charlotte. 'You have a house of your own, so I suppose you must be some sort of foreman.'

'*Mais ou menos*—more or less.' Roberto looked away, out across the expanse of grass, which stretched mile upon mile until it met the edge of the sky. 'A great number of the cattle you saw belong to Estancia Velha. There are fences which mark the boundaries and grazing areas, but perhaps you could not see them from the air.'

'I had no idea it would be so immense.' Charlotte eyed him curiously. 'How many cattle do you look after personally?'

'Enough to keep me sufficiently busy, I promise.'

There was silence while they finished their coffee, and Charlotte searched for ways to broach the reason for her presence in this neat, empty little house, so far from anywhere that they could have been alone in the world, except for the faint sound of music somewhere in the background.

'Teresa has a radio in her room outside at the back of the house,' he said abruptly. 'I trust it does not disturb you.'

'Not in the least.'

'Is your father's leg now recovered?'

'Yes. He's had a lot of physiotherapy and does exercises, and so on. He doesn't even limp now.'

'I am glad.' He eyed her through his cigar smoke. 'So. All is now back to normal for you, Charlotte.'

Is it likely I'd come half-way round the world to see you if it were, she thought bitterly. 'It will be,' she said aloud, 'when my father finally owns the land you have for sale.'

'And you are such a good daughter you come many thousands of miles to ensure your father gains his heart's desire!' He shrugged. 'When I have a daughter I shall consider myself fortunate to command such loyalty.'

The thought of Roberto fathering a daughter caused Charlotte such unexpected pain that she breathed in sharply and he straightened, frowning, moving to her side.

'What is it? You are ill, Charlotte?'

'No—no. I burnt my tongue on the coffee,' she said and flushed at the quizzical look he gave her as he resumed his hat.

'I regret I cannot stay to lunch with you,' he said, formal once more. 'Teresa will cook whatever you choose from the refrigerator, after which I suggest you rest. You must be suffering from jet-lag, *não é*? I apologise for adding to your journey.'

'Not at all,' she answered, equally formal. 'It's been *such* an interesting experience. For some reason I assumed you were a dairy farmer, you see. I had no idea you worked on a cattle ranch.'

'There are many things we did not learn about each other, Charlotte.' His eyes were sardonic. 'Our—acquaintance was cut so brutally short, was it not?'

Charlotte eyed him with hostility. 'Yes. It was. The prospect of imminent assault does tend to speed the departing female guest.'

He stiffened, his face taut. 'For that I apologise. But do not forget that I had just suffered deep disillusion at your hands——'

'And decided a spot of rape would even the score?' she asked scornfully.

Roberto pulled his hat low over eyes which glittered at her darkly from under the brim. 'Ah, but in the end, Charlotte,' he said in a voice which made her shiver, 'I doubt very much that it would have been rape.' And he turned on his spurred heel and strode to the jeep without a backward glance.

CHAPTER SIX

CHARLOTTE fumed with frustration as she watched the jeep out of sight, angry at her lack of choice to do anything but stay where she was until Roberto Monteiro chose to honour her with his presence again.

'*Dona Carlota.*'

Charlotte turned to find the maid standing in the doorway, and smiled encouragingly.

'*A senhora quer almoçar?*' Teresa made eating motions by way of illustration and Charlotte nodded, smiling. Having lunch would pass the time, if nothing else.

By means of much hand-waving Charlotte was able to convey her approval of the proposed menu of omelette and salad and went off to have a wash and change her black suit and silk shirt for denims and white sweatshirt. Her suitcase had already been unpacked in the small, spartan bedroom, and all her clothes were either hanging in the wardrobe or folded neatly in the chest. Charlotte looked round curiously, but found no traces of Roberto's occupancy. There seemed to be nothing in the entire house that belonged to him.

As she went back to the living-room Charlotte frowned, puzzled, as she realised there were no pictures on the white walls, no ornaments, nothing to soften the bright impersonal bareness of the house. She shrugged and seated herself at the table before a puffy golden omelette as good as anything she had ever tasted. It was a little difficult to pass on her appreciation to Teresa with her limited vocabulary, but the girl obviously understood, smiling her pleasure at Charlotte's enthusiasm for the meal. Afterwards Teresa indicated shyly that the *senhora* lie down on the bed and rest, and Charlotte found she was quite happy to do as the girl suggested, surprised to find she was tired again. I must stop sleeping so much, was her last coherent thought. Not much point in coming to Brazil if I don't keep my eyes open at least half the time I'm here.

Charlotte woke to the sound of voices and horses' hooves receding into the distance. Roberto? She sprang from the bed to peer through the window, but it was already quite dark and there was nothing to see other than a glow from the region of the outhouse. Charlotte turned away hurriedly as she saw that she had slept for hours. She pulled on a dressing-gown and espadrilles and went in search of Teresa, who was in the kitchen, surrounded by pots and pans, singing softly in company with her small transistor radio.

'*Boa tarde*, Teresa,' said Charlotte, smiling. 'Senhor Monteiro?'

'*Boa tarde, senhora.*' The girl shook her head. *Senhor Monteiro vem as oito horas.*' She held up eight fingers in confirmation, and waved at her preparations. '*Para jantar com a senhora.*'

Charlotte nodded, enlightened. So Roberto would be here for dinner at eight whether she approved of the arrangement or not. But who had just ridden away? With a little mime and much mixing of tenses she managed to ask who had just visited the house.

Teresa smiled, blushing, explaining that the visitor had been Paulinho, her *noivo*, who worked for the *Patrão*.

Charlotte went off to have a bath, wondering if she were likely to meet this *'Patrão'* person everyone talked of before she left. She pictured him as a Zeus-like figure, overseeing his employees like a deity from afar, and grinned at the idea as she washed her hair and towelled it and brushed it until it shone like copper silk. She left it loose to finish drying while she slid into a crêpe-de-Chine teddy, and a narrow-skirted dress in honey-coloured cotton jersey printed in white, chosen for its uncrushable qualities. She added Mrs Presteigne's pearls and took some time over making up her face before beginning on her hair. Half-way through the process of coiling and pinning Charlotte changed her mind and left it loose. Roberto liked it that way, and knowing that he did would give her confidence. And if Roberto Monteiro chose to think she was the kind of female who used her charms to gain her own ends—or her father's—he was welcome to do so.

She looked about her thoughtfully. If this rather claustrophobic little house was all he owned by way of a home, no wonder he had been eager to get her over here to clinch the deal, because no doubt his *'Patrão'* wouldn't give him time off for another holiday in England so soon, even if Roberto could afford it, which seemed unlikely. It was significant that he had made no further mention of paying her travelling expenses once she had written to say her father would foot the bill for her flight and hotel.

Charlotte was sitting reading on the veranda when she heard the sound of a jeep and voices, and then footsteps approaching from the rear of the house. As Roberto came in sight she put down her book without haste and rose to her feet.

'Good evening,' she said quietly.

Roberto said nothing for a moment, his eyes on the long red fall of hair. 'Good evening, Charlotte,' he said at last, his accent very pronounced. 'I trust you are rested.' His rather startling gaucho costume had been replaced by conservative white shirt and dark trousers, which for some reason served only to make him even more attractive, thought his guest with resentment.

'I slept for hours.' Charlotte smiled politely. 'I seem to need far more sleep here than at home.'

'It is quite normal.' He glanced through the open door of the living-room, where the table was laid for two. 'I trust you are as hungry as I am. It has been a long day.'

Teresa served them spiced tomato soup, followed by the melodramatic appearance of two great skewers of sizzling beef which she set in the racks in front of each plate.

'My goodness,' said Charlotte, impressed. 'That's a lot of meat. I was wondering about the little racks.'

'This is the more civilised way of eating *churrasco*—barbecue.' Roberto smiled as Teresa appeared with a basket of hot bread and a salad of lettuce and peppers and tomatoes, with circular slices of a white vegetable new to Charlotte.

'What is this?' she asked, tasting it.

'*Palmito*. Heart of palm. But did you not try a *churrasco* in the Capitão Rodrigo restaurant in the hotel last night? They serve the best beef in Brazil in Port Alegre.'

'I ate in my room,' said Charlotte, slicing off a piece of meat as Roberto demonstrated. It was wonderfully juicy, with the unique flavour achieved by grilling over an open charcoal fire.

'Teresa cooked this outside. I brought her *noivo*, Paulinho, to share her meal. I trust you do not object?' Roberto helped her to some of the salad.

'Of course not. Will he stay here tonight?'

Robert looked disapproving. 'No! He will ride back with me later.'

'I was merely enquiring so I'd know who was around.' Charlotte drank some of the wine in her glass, which was fairly thick and inexpensive, as was the pottery they were eating from. 'This house seems fairly isolated.'

'If you wish, Teresa may sleep in the house and Paulinho in her room outside,' said Roberto at once, and eyed her questioningly. 'But I assure you that you are perfectly safe. Otherwise you would not be here. I do not expose my guests to danger.'

'I'm not in the least nervous,' Charlotte assured him and changed the subject. 'You mentioned a bereavement. I trust it was no one very close to you.'

'Let us not talk of it,' he said shortly. 'You like the meat, Charlotte?'

'It's quite wonderful.' She eyed the half-eaten contents of the vertical skewer and shrugged. 'But somehow I don't think I'll manage any more.'

'You have eaten very little.'

He was right. Charlotte had forgotten how much Roberto Monteiro's physical presence affected her. Just sitting opposite him again, with the candle-light glinting on his close-curling black hair, was having a detrimental effect on her appetite. 'I ate a large lunch,' she said apologetically. 'Teresa's a good cook.'

Roberto seemed to have no further interest in his own meal and rang the small silver bell beside him. Teresa came in with a bowl of fresh figs and a pitcher of cream and removed the remains of the main course in smiling silence, thanking Roberto when he told her to go off and enjoy her own dinner with Paulinho.

Charlotte enjoyed the figs, but was glad, never-theless, to leave the candlelit room for the veranda, which was in semi-darkness, illumined by only a single, glass-shaded lantern at the far end, away from the small table and the two rattan chairs. She shivered suddenly in the darkness, the evening air cooler than expected.

'You are cold,' said Roberto and touched her arm, and instantly they both shied away as if they had been stung.

'I—I'll get something to put on,' muttered Charlotte and fled to the bedroom, searching for the big cashmere square brought to use as a wrap. She took it out of a drawer with shaking hands and swathed it round herself, cursing the weakness of her own flesh. Her brain might be angry with Roberto Monteiro, but the rest of her was all too obviously delighted to be with him again.

When she joined him on the veranda Roberto was smoking a cigar and looking out at the stars which hung like great diamond pendants in the black night sky.

'Coffee?' asked Charlotte, and seated herself in front of the tray Teresa had brought in during her absence.

'Thank you.'

Charlotte was grateful for something to do, since the atmosphere between them was still uncomfortably tense. She made herself concentrate on filling the tiny cups with the strong black liquid, adding sugar to Roberto's, not pretending this time that she had forgotten how he liked it.

'Shall we be able to get the contracts signed tonight?' she asked, determined to put things on a businesslike footing.

'If you wish.' He ground out his cigar. 'You will like to know that I rang your parents earlier. The *Patrão* gave me permission to telephone from the house to say you were safe at Estancia Velha.'

Charlotte looked at him in surprise. 'Why, thank you, that was very thoughtful. And please thank your employer for allowing you to ring them. What did they say?'

'They sent their love, naturally. I explained the situation to them and said you would contact them on your return to Porto Alegre.'

'You're very kind.' Charlotte noticed that Teresa had cleared away in the living-room, and stood up, picking up the briefcase she had brought from the bedroom. 'Shall we go inside and get on with it, then? I've no wish to trespass on your hospitality any more than absolutely necessary.'

Roberto turned on the main lights in the living-room and motioned her to the sofa. '*Por que,*

Charlotte? Why are you so eager to leave Estancia Velha as soon as you arrive? Would you not like to see something of my—my country now you are here?'

She shook her head as he sat beside her, busying herself with extracting the necessary documents from her briefcase. 'I think it's best I go back as soon as possible.'

'I had hoped you would stay at least another day. The *Patrão* wishes you to dine at the house before you leave.' Roberto took the contract from her and began to read.

Charlotte felt taken aback. She had been curious to meet this *Patrão* of Roberto's before she left, admittedly, but an invitation to dinner was unexpected. 'Do you dine with him often?' she asked curiously.

'*Sim,*' said Roberto absently, concentrating on the legal jargon he was trying to unravel. He looked up in appeal. 'I find this unintelligible, Charlotte. I read colloquial English well enough, but I do not understand these legal terms.'

'Very well.' She leaned closer to look at the pages he held and found they were shaking slightly in his grasp. She brushed back a loose strand of hair and looked up at him questioningly, her breath catching in her throat as she met the look in his eyes.

'Charlotte,' he said harshly. 'Move away from me. Please!'

She drew back hurriedly, her teeth catching in her lower lip, and he uttered a choked sound and dropped the papers on the floor as his hands reached out and caught hers.

'Do not——' he began, but never finished what he began to say as he pulled her to him and kissed her hungrily and Charlotte gasped and responded helplessly, as though that final scene at Presteigne House had never happened.

'Amada,' he muttered thickly, holding her so tightly she feared for her ribs.

'The contract——' she protested breathlessly, and he thrust his hands through her hair, holding her head still so that he could look deep into her eyes.

'To hell with the contract, *querida*. I will sign my soul away if you wish, only let me hold you, kiss you as I have dreamed of doing all these weeks.'

'But will it stop at kisses?' she asked shakily. 'Millie Sutton's not here to come to my rescue this time!'

He shook her slightly. 'I promise. Word of a Monteiro!' He drew back a little, his eyes narrowing. 'Or is it that you will only give me my reward once I have signed my Yorkshire acres over to you, Miss Charlotte Mercer?'

She stiffened and pushed him away in a fury, her eyes flashing fire. 'That's a despicable thing to say, particularly when you got me over here because you you obviously need the money very badly.' She waved a hand disparagingly at the small room. 'It's not much like Presteigne House, is it?'

Roberto sprang to his feet, the hauteur on his face almost menacing as he drew himself to his full height. 'So. You have interest only in men who live in large houses, who have much money! Is that why you are still *solteira*—and *virgem*, if you can be believed. Perhaps the only suitors for your hand have been too poor to be granted such a great favour, *não é verdade*?'

Charlotte shook back her hair, trembling with rage. 'How dare you? When I marry—*if* I marry—it will be for love, not money.' She glared up into his angry eyes. 'To think that when I met you I really imagined I had found love! While you found it only too easy to believe I was offering myself as bait to get your miserable bit of land for my father. If I were going to sell myself, the price would be a lot higher than a couple hundred acres, I assure you!'

'Exactly how many acres would be necessary?' he asked unforgivably, and Charlotte went white with temper. She bent suddenly and picked up the contract.

'Are you going to sign this or not?' She hurled the words at him and Roberto's hands clenched by his side, the corners of his flexible mouth compressed in fury.

'*Pois é*—it would be a great pity to have you come all this way for nothing,' he snarled, and Charlotte dived for the briefcase and took out a pen.

'Right! Let me translate it into simple terms even *you* can understand.'

'Do not trouble yourself.' Roberto seized the contract and sat at the table, scrawling his long, bold signature with a force that almost punctured the thick legal document. 'Now you sign,' he commanded, but Charlotte shook her head.

'I need your signature on the copy first. Then I'll countersign both and that's it, except for the bit I've been waiting for.'

He scribbled his signature a second time before raising his eyebrows imperiously. 'And which "bit" is that?'

'You'll see.' Charlotte signed both contracts and took a cheque from the inner compartment of the briefcase. She added her signature to her father's on the cheque and took a deep breath of fierce satisfaction. 'There you are, Robert Monteiro. Take your wretched money. I wish you joy of it!' And she threw the cheque in his outraged face and ran to her bedroom and slid home the bolt on the door.

CHAPTER SEVEN

SAFE inside the room, Charlotte leaned against the door, breathing raggedly, her heart banging against her ribs, certain Roberto would follow her and hammer for admittance. When it became clear, after a time, that he was going to do nothing of the kind, she sat down on the edge of the bed feeling faintly ridiculous. And where, she wondered bleakly, was the great surge of elation she had looked forward to with such anticipation? Like Roberto, it was conspicuous by its absence. She listened intently, hearing the faint, distant music of Teresa's radio, but no footsteps outside her door, nor Roberto's voice demanding entrance.

Charlotte turned over abruptly, and lay face down on the bed, feeling utterly deflated and depressed. It had been a long way to come, and a lot of money spent on her journey, just for a few short moments of triumph to pay back Roberto Monteiro for casting aspersions on her morals. She had been fired for weeks with the desire to humiliate him, to throw money at him like an empress tossing largesse to a beggar. And now she felt no satisfaction at all. Nothing. Only a strong desire to cry her eyes out and rush back to him to assure him she didn't mean any of it, that he could be as poor as a church mouse as far as she was concerned. It would make no difference to her feelings for him. She tensed, her head raised. Voices were saying goodbye as the

jeep started up, then drove off. Had Roberto just
gone without another word, now he had his beloved money safe in his hot little hand? Only his
hands weren't hot. Or little. They were long and
hard and cool, and she longed for their touch so
much she could hardly bear it. Charlotte buried her
face in the pillow and wept scalding, racking tears,
abandoned completely to the grief that rushed over
her like a black, engulfing tide.

It was much later when she dragged herself off
the bed and changed her clothes for silk pyjamas
and thin Swiss cotton robe. Listlessly she thrust her
feet into espadrilles and pushed her untidy hair
away from her face, aware of a raging thirst. Since
Teresa was likely to be in bed by this time, Charlotte
felt safe in raiding the refrigerator for whatever cold
drink it contained. She unbolted the door and went
wearily along the little hall to the kitchen. The outer
door was closed and all seemed quiet as Charlotte
opened the refrigerator, which was well stocked with
fruit juices and mineral water, as well as the ubiqui-
tous Coca Cola and tonic water. She decided on the
latter, glad of its refreshing bitterness as she drank
an entire glassful almost without pause.

'You were very thirsty!'

Charlotte whirled round, staring in numb dismay
at Roberto, who was leaning in the doorway. His
face was sombre as his eyes took in her swollen
eyelids and shiny pink nose.

'You have been weeping, Charlotte.'

She was at a loss. 'I thought you'd gone,' she
said at last, dismayed to find her voice so hoarse
it was almost unrecognisable.

'I gave Paulinho permission to take Teresa in the jeep to the house. Her mother is the cook there.'

'Oh.'

Roberto straightened. 'Do not disturb yourself. He will bring her back later.'

Charlotte couldn't find the energy to be disturbed about anything for the moment. Her capacity for emotion of any kind seemed to have drowned in the flood of tears.

'Why didn't you say you were still here?' she asked dully.

'I thought my presence would not please you.' There was a tinge of irony in his voice.

'Whether you go or stay is of no interest to me, I assure you,' she said, with a shameless disregard for the truth, and felt a little better as she saw her little barb find its target with precision.

Roberto gave her an ironic little bow. 'You are expert at insolence, Miss Charlotte Mercer.'

She shrugged indifferently, and turned away, then hesitated and turned back to him. 'How soon may I leave, please?'

'Not for at least two days. I regret the inconvenience. The aeroplane is undergoing repair.'

Charlotte stared at him in dismay. 'Is there no other form of transport?'

'We are a long way from the nearest railroad, alas. You would be well advised to wait until Jorge Pires flies you back to Porto Alegre.' Roberto's tone was so emphatic Charlotte's shoulders slumped in defeat.

'But what on earth will I do with myself until then?' The question was almost a wail, to her mortification, and Roberto's eyes softened.

'Come,' he said, holding out his hand. 'Let us sit in the *sala* until Teresa returns, and we shall discuss ways of passing your time as agreeably as possible while you are at Estancia Velha.' He smiled coaxingly. 'Is it truly impossible for us to be friends, Charlotte, now all is settled?'

Charlotte eyed the outstretched hand, that long, brown hand she had just been thinking about, and gave an unsteady sigh as she put hers into it. 'I suppose not, Roberto. But I think I'd better get dressed again.'

He lifted her hand to his lips and kissed it, his eyes glinting up at her in the way that had haunted so many of her dreams. 'I agree—wholeheartedly.'

Charlotte smiled faintly and freed her hand. 'Five minutes, then.' She took very little longer to splash cold water on her face, and to resume her discarded dress, feeling it would look a lot better to Teresa if Senhor Monteiro's guest was not only fully dressed when the maid returned, but dressed in the same clothes worn to dine earlier.

Roberto sprang to his feet as Charlotte rejoined him, smiling at her with the warmth she remembered so well.

'You look better, Charlotte. Your so beautiful self again. And now we have completed the transaction to your satisfaction, and you have achieved your object in travelling so far, let us drink a toast to the successful culmination of your father's dream of a country club for your town of Prestleigh.'

'By all means,' agreed Charlotte, and eyed the pale liquid in the glass he handed her. 'Champagne?'

'*Pois é*. Champagne, what else?'

'Do you drink much of it here, then?'

He shook his head solemnly, waving a hand at their surroundings. 'Does it appear that I do?'

Charlotte bit her lip. 'I apologise. I was very rude earlier on.'

Roberto leaned back in his chair, his eyes bright with amusement. 'No, Charlotte. You spoke with candour—is that the right word?'

'It's a lot better than rudeness!' She smiled and raised her glass. 'So—here's to Presteigne Country Club.'

He leaned forward and touched his glass to hers. 'Presteigne Country Club. May it flourish and be successful.' He drained his glass, then refilled it, and topped up Charlotte's. 'And now another toast. To the future.'

Charlotte looked at him warily, then smiled. 'Why not? To the future.'

Roberto asked permission to smoke, then leaned back, relaxed. 'Do you ride, Charlotte?'

She nodded with enthusiasm. 'Since I was a child. I had a pony of my own when I was young, but these days I just hire a hack from the local riding-stables whenever I can.'

'Then since you cannot leave tomorrow, would you like to ride with me, allow me to show you something of life here in Estancia Velha?'

Charlotte's eyes lit up. 'Oh yes, please! I'd love to——' she checked herself, trying to hold on to the impersonal manner she had been at pains to establish, but it was impossible. The silken cord of rapport was there between them strong as ever, and she knew perfectly well that Roberto felt it as strongly as she did, that he was no more indifferent to her than she was to him. Several weeks of separation had done nothing to lessen the pull between them, in spite of their quarrel. 'I like this enormous country of yours,' she went on. 'What little I've seen of it, at least. And when I'm back in Prestleigh it will be pleasant to picture you in your own surroundings.'

'Pleasant,' repeated Roberto without enthusiasm. 'A lukewarm word.'

Charlotte chose to ignore it. 'Do I need special clothes? I brought some denims; will they do?'

'*Perfeitamente*. Have you a thick sweater also? It is cold in the mornings.'

'Yes. And a cotton windcheater.' Charlotte glanced at her feet. 'No boots, though.'

'I shall bring some in the morning. They may be a little large, but they will do, I think.' Roberto paused, his eyes questioning. 'You are no longer quite so unhappy, Charlotte? Your tears gave me much distress.'

'They didn't do me much good either.' She pulled a face. 'I hardly ever cry, you know. Anyway, I'm fine again now.'

'I am glad.' He rose to his feet, hesitating. 'Charlotte——' The sound of the returning jeep interrupted him and he shrugged philosophically. 'Paulinho returns with Teresa. I must go.'

'So soon?' Charlotte said without thinking, and flushed. 'I mean, it's not late.'

'It is for me. We go early to our beds here—and leave them early also!' His smile was sudden and oddly comradely. 'I shall call for you at six, Miss Mercer.'

'Six!' Charlotte's eyes widened as she scrambled to her feet. 'In that case, on your bike, Senhor Monteiro, I'd better get to bed right away!'

'Bike?' he laughed. 'No, no. I use only the jeep.'

'And your horse!'

A shadow crossed his face. 'And my horse,' he agreed. '*Até amanha,* Charlotte. *Amanha cedo*—which means early!'

Charlotte was up and dressed well before six, grateful for the coffee and rolls Teresa had ready for her. As she drank the strong black brew Charlotte felt excitement bubble up inside her, mixed with apprehension about her ability to cope with the type of mount Roberto and all the other men had been riding the day before. The horses at Estancia Velha were a smallish, rough-coated breed, stockier than the type of hack she rode at weekends in Prestleigh, presumably suited to the requirements of the cattle country she had seen from the air. By the time I come back tonight, I'll have seen it all first-hand, she thought, as she shrugged on a blue fisherman's jersey. When she was back home again she would have a clear picture of how and where Roberto Monteiro spent his days. Her face sobered. Estancia Velha was a long, long way from Yorkshire, and now the Presteigne estate was off his hands Roberto would have no reason for visiting Prestleigh again unless . . .

Charlotte blocked off that train of thought, and busied herself with weaving her hair into one thick braid to hang tidily out of the way. As she was securing the end with an elastic band she heard the sound of hoofbeats in the distance, and ran outside to the veranda, staring into the distance in the soft morning light, as Roberto came into view on horseback, dressed in gaucho fashion once more, but with a heavy suede jerkin on top. He led a compact little grey horse on a rein, and smiled in greeting, his teeth a brief flash of white under the hatbrim as he dismounted, tethering the two horses to a nearby rail before striding towards her, hand outstretched.

'*Bom dia,* Charlotte. You are ready, I see.'

Charlotte's answering smile was smug as she took his hand. 'Did you think I wouldn't be, then?'

Roberto turned to unstrap a package from his horse, then presented it to Charlotte with a flourish. 'These were my mother's boots. I hope they may fit. Also a hat. You will need it.'

The hat was a replica of his own, and the boots were of soft, wrinkled leather, carefully waxed and preserved. Charlotte sat down on the step and tried them on, smiling happily as she stood up again. The boots were on the loose side, and shorter than the type she wore at home, but otherwise perfect for a day in the saddle, as was the hat. Charlotte clapped it on her red head and laughed up at Roberto.

'There!' She twirled round in front of him. 'Will I do?'

'Oh, yes.' There was a very gratifying huskiness to his voice. 'You will do. Now let me introduce you to Filinha.' He led her over to the horses and Charlotte patted the little grey and told her how pretty she was and how well they would get on together, then inspected the saddle, which was very different from the type used at Prestleigh Stables.

Filinha's saddle had no pommel or cantle; it was a simple sandwich of leather pads and woollen blankets, with a thick sheepskin on top.

Roberto buckled circular spurs to Charlotte's soft leather boots, handed her the reins and gave her a leg up into the saddle. Charlotte settled herself easily, leaning forward to gentle the horse while Roberto adjusted her stirrups, grinning up at her.

'You may like to know you are fortunate to have stirrups, Charlotte. At one time the gaucho rode barefoot, gripping leather straps between the toes for the balance.'

Charlotte grinned back as Roberto swung up on his own mount. 'Thank the lord for progress, then.'

'I am not certain I agree.' Roberto urged his horse forward and Charlotte followed suit on Filinha. Both saddle and gait felt a little strange at first, but as they settled into a trot Charlotte relaxed and began to enjoy herself.

'Don't you approve of progress then, Roberto?'

He shrugged, settling his hat lower over his eyes. '*Pois é*—in some ways. For us here, in Estancia Velha, I like things the way they are.' He waved a gloved hand towards the horizon, where a long streak of brown marked the presence of the herd. 'Sometimes I feel I am a vanishing breed. In the past few decades industry has begun to predominate over agriculture in my country. Here, we go on as we have always done, driving our herds from one pasture to another, but other *fazendeiros*—ranchers—have introduced different strains of cattle, and some resort to scientific feeding rather than natural pasturage. Others turn their land over to the cultivation of the soya bean.' He sighed.

'Perhaps one day it will be the same here, who knows?'

Charlotte took firmer control of the reins, as Filinha showed a skittish tendency to pirouette. 'But you prefer the status quo, Roberto.'

'This is *minha terra*, Charlotte, my land.' His voice throbbed with a possessive ring as he swept a hand to encompass the rolling green infinity about them. 'A Brazilian is not afraid to claim he is *macho*, that he will fight for the land and way of life that is his.'

Charlotte was stirred by his words, despite their unashamed drama. 'Do all the other men feel the same?'

'Other men?'

She gestured towards the riders they could see in the distance, strung out along the great moving mass of cattle. 'Your fellow gauchos.'

Roberto smiled exuberently. 'Of course! We take great pride in our stamina, our horsemanship, the *liberdade de espirito*——' He checked himself ruefully. '*Perdoneme*. I am trying to say we have a freedom of the spirit, a loyalty to each other, which is very important in the long hours and days we must spend together out here in the *campo*.'

Charlotte nodded in understanding, her excitement mounting as they came in earshot of the mighty bellowing herd as the encircling horsemen and dogs drove the cattle on, herding them through gates in the line of fences she could now see demarcating the pastures. 'What a sight,' she shouted over the noise. 'How many cattle are in this lot?'

'Several hundred head,' yelled Roberto, and moved his horse nearer, so that they rode knee to knee. 'Stay close, Charlotte. Do not venture far from me.'

'I shan't!' she assured him, and kept her word as they followed the herd at a respectful distance once the last stragglers had been rounded up by means of much flapping of the long white scarves tied to the wrists of some of the men.

'The herd goes to pastures far beyond here,' said Roberto. 'Are you tired, Charlotte, or do you wish to ride with it for a while?'

'I'm not in the least tired!' Her eyes flashed indignantly. 'I thought I was out for the day. Besides, shouldn't you be doing your bit with the others?'

'The *Patrão* says I must take good care of the beautiful English visitor. I am excused more onerous duties today.'

Charlotte's eyebrows rose. 'That's very gracious of him. But who told him anything about my looks, I wonder?'

'It was I, *carinha*.' Black eyes met brown under the hatbrims, and Charlotte's were the first to look away. 'Come,' said Roberto, 'let us put on a little speed. When we reach the *missão* we shall stop for coffee.'

'*Missão?*' queried Charlotte, spurring on Filinha to keep up with Roberto.

'The ruins of a Jesuit mission lie a few kilometres to the south,' he said over his shoulder.

Once they were well clear of the herd it was exhilarating to gallop through the bright morning sunshine over a landscape unpopulated by anything but the grass and sky, with the muted thunder of the herd reminding them of the cattle's presence to the rear. Charlotte was breathless when, at last, she caught sight of curving stone arches and ruined walls on the skyline. When they reached the ruins Roberto dismounted, and Charlotte brought Filinha to a halt.

'We shall rest here, Charlotte,' he said as he took her reins. 'Can you dismount unaided?'

For answer Charlotte swung one leg over the saddle and slid to the ground, giving a little yelp as her knees buckled slightly. Roberto laughed as he caught her by the elbow with one hand, holding on to the reins of both horses with the other. '*Cuidado, carinha*. Have you not ridden for a while?'

'Not as far as this,' she admitted, straightening as some of the men rode up to join them. Roberto tethered the horses and began a series of introductions. The men greeted Charlotte with an endearing mixture of courtesy and shyness, and she shook hands with them all, hoping she would remember which was which among Geraldo, Valdemar, Jango, José and Virgilinho. The others had remained with the temporarily stationed herd, Roberto told her, and spread a rug for her on the grass, while his companions got a fire going with the speed of long practice. It was only a matter of minutes before water was boiling to provide the guest with coffee and to make the *maté*, the bitter herbal tea Roberto, like the others, drank from a gourd through a utensil which fascinated Charlotte. Roberto handed it to her, explaining that although shaped like a spoon, it functioned like the everyday straw used by children to drink the fizzy drinks they loved.

'See,' said Roberto. 'The bowl is pierced with many holes so that the *maté* leaves are not drawn with the liquid through the hollow stem from the *chimarrão*—the gourd.'

'May I try some?' she asked.

'I do not have another——'

'Yours will do.'

Under the amused, friendly gaze of his *companheiros* Roberto was silent, but his eyes were eloquent as he held out his gourd to her. Charlotte's colour deepened as she dipped the perforated spoon into the gourd and bent her head to suck up the *maté* through the hollow stem. The scalding mouthful of bitter liquid burnt her tongue and sent an involuntary shudder through her as she swallowed it and drew away, making a face at the others in pantomime of her reaction to the flavour. She waved away the gourd emphatically.

'*Não, obrigada—café, faz favor!*'

The men roared with laughter, and Virgilinho, the youngest and best looking, sprang to refill her mug from the metal coffee-pot balanced on the embers of the fire. Charlotte thanked him gracefully and he gave her a smiling bow before stamping out the fire and preparing to depart with the others.

'You really wish to go on?' asked Roberto when they were alone.

'Of course I do!' Charlotte smiled at him and jumped to her feet.

Roberto put a hand on her arm, his eyes very serious as they looked down into hers. 'While we are still alone, Charlotte, let us talk a little of last night. You were very angry when you threw your cheque at me. The anger—it was all for that night at Presteigne House when I so stupidly lost my head?'

Charlotte looked away, unwilling to discuss her thirst for revenge, which seemed very petty out here in the almost intimidating emptiness of the pampas. 'That last night in Prestleigh I was cut to the quick because you could even consider me capable of using myself as lure to get you to sign the contract,' she said quietly. 'It was only later that I became angry. So when your letter arrived, asking me to come here in person to finalise the sale of the Presteigne estate, I jumped at the opportunity to throw the money in your face.'

'As you did!'

'Yes.' Charlotte smiled ruefully. 'I really thought I'd feel pleased, satisfied...'

'Instead of which you wept.' Roberto lifted her hand and kissed it. 'Can you forgive me for *my* sins, Charlotte, if I forgive your natural desire for revenge?'

They stood very still for some moments, looking at each other in sober silence. Then Charlotte smiled, and Roberto's black, expressive eyes lit with relief.

'I vote we start with a clean sheet,' she said cheerfully.

'With no sins written upon it!' He laughed and tossed her up onto Filinha's saddle, then swung up on his own mount. '*Vamos,* then, Charlotte. Let's go.'

Charlotte enjoyed herself to the full during the next few hours as they followed the slow-moving herd with the others, stopping later for a brief, simple lunch of bread and cheese and *maté*, and

more coffee for Charlotte. She felt as though a great
load had rolled from her shoulders, leaving her free
to enjoy the sun on her face, the freedom of the
vast landscape, and, by no means least, Roberto's
company. He warned her that soon after they ate
it would be necessary for the two of them to turn
back, leaving the others to continue the drive to the
new pasture, a journey of at least a night and
another day.

'I never imagined it would be so immense,' said
Charlotte as she remounted Filinha. 'How you must
have laughed at me, Roberto, when I talked about
your "cows".'

He laid his hand on his heart, his eyes dancing.
'I swear I did not!'

'H'm.' Charlotte was sceptical as they resumed
their progress. 'Tell me exactly what you do. I
mean, you can't just ride about with your cattle
like this.'

'*Não, senhora,* we don't. A gaucho must be
capable of many skills. I notch ears, brand
haunches, dose the sick cows.' He frowned,
searching for the English words. 'I take off the
horns of the calves; de-horn. Is that right?' He hesitated. 'Also I must *castrar*—er, castrate the young
bulls.'

Charlotte pulled a face. 'Poor things!'

'It is necessary, believe me!'

'Tell me why you wear those beads, Roberto.'

He glanced down at the black discs, which were
strung on a plaited leather thong. 'It is how I make
the *conta*—the tally, I think you say. Each bead
represent fifty beasts.' He grinned. 'Did you think
they were worn for ornament!'

'Your entire outfit is sheer ornament!' Charlotte eased the denim hugging her thighs. 'I envy you those loose breeches. They must be very comfortable.'

'The *bombachas* are very practical for long hours in the saddle.' Roberto looked at this watch and frowned. 'Come, we must go, Charlotte. It is later than I thought.'

Charlotte was reluctant to part company with the mighty herd and its picturesque attendants. She rode up to each one in turn to make her farewells, and as she reached Geraldo, the oldest of them, he shot a questioning glance at Roberto, then as the latter nodded the weathered, elderly horseman put his fingers in his mouth and Charlotte gaped, open-mouthed at the moving billow of white, which swept like a foaming breaker through the ocean of brown as the white Hereford face on every cow looked up in answer to the whistle, then down once more as the gauchos urged them on.

Charlotte was rendered temporarily speechless by the spectacle, her eyes shining like lamps under the upturned brim of her borrowed hat.

'Senhor Geraldo,' she gasped as the final flicker of white disappeared. *'Muita obrigada.'* She hesitated, searching for a word. *'Maravilhosa!'* she said in triumph, beaming at him.

'De nada, senhora!' The man returned the smile, touched his hat and joined his fellows.

'That was entirely for your benefit,' said Roberto, who was stowing away an extra saddlebag brought by one of the men. 'Normally that is done just before the light goes, when the herd is settled for the night, so that we may make the *conta*, and see that all are safe. Since we must return now, Geraldo put on his little show especially for you.'

Charlotte was wistful. 'If only I'd had my camera, Roberto! I left it behind because I was in such a hurry to be ready when you came for me.'

He brought his horse close, and touched a hand to hers. 'Then you must ride the herd again, *carinha*, and I shall get my "cows" to perform for you once more.'

Charlotte laughed and shook her head. 'I wish I could, but I must go home soon, get back to my job. Heaven knows what havoc my father's creating in my nice orderly office while I'm away.'

Roberto moved away, his face clouding. 'I wish so much that you would stay, Charlotte—at least until you have seen more of my—my country.'

'I wish I could, too. I love it here. The people are so charming and friendly——'

Roberto bowed, his eyes gleaming. *'Muito obrigado, senhora!'*

She laughed, and swept an arm about her. 'I like the actual terrain here, too, the space, the peace. I never thought I'd find a place to rival my native dales, but if any place does, this is it.'

'You do not find it lonely out here in the *campo*?' asked Roberto swiftly.

Charlotte smoothed Filinha's pale, curving neck thoughtfully. 'Not in the least,' she said slowly, and looked away into the distance, where an occasional group of eucalyptus trees provided the only breaks in the grassland stretching to the horizon. 'I suppose I ought to find the emptiness intimidating, but I don't.' She kept her eyes straight ahead, not wanting Roberto to realise that her reason for loving everything in this corner of the earth was simple. It was where Roberto Gaspar Monteiro had his home. A place where, she now knew beyond all possibility of doubt, her heart had found its home for all time.

CHAPTER EIGHT

THEY rode on in complete harmony, with nothing to break the silence except the creak and jangle of the harness and the occasional snort from their mounts. Charlotte was glad of the lack of conversation, since her entire concentration was fast becoming centred on hiding her increasing discomfort. Eventually Roberto called a halt as they reached a group of trees overlooking a small stream.

'Time to eat, Charlotte.' He tethered their horses and held up his arms, his brows meeting when he saw how much she needed his help to dismount.

'I'm a bit stiff,' she admitted with a tired smile, and yawned a little. Roberto pushed her hat back and examined her face. 'You are exhausted, *carinha*. I was a fool to let you ride so far. Come, sit down on the rug and I shall make a fire and cook your dinner.'

Charlotte chuckled as she stumbled awkwardly after him. 'You mean you can cook?'

He shook out the rug, looking smug. '*Pois é.* Every gaucho can cook. Who else is there to do it when we ride herd?'

'I hadn't thought of that!' Charlotte made her way slowly over to the trees, in need of few necessary moments of privacy behind their convenient screen while Roberto gathered wood for their fire. It was some time before she returned, biting her lip as her legs and back grew stiffer by the minute. Roberto looked up anxiously from the fire.

'Come and warm yourself, Charlotte, while I prepare our *churrasco*.'

She flopped down gratefully and reached out her hands to the flames while Roberto took two pieces of meat from the extra saddlebag and threaded them on metal skewers which he planted in the glowing heart of the fire.

'You're amazing, Roberto! Where did they come from?'

'I begged them from Valdemar, also your coffee-pot, in case we—we were late for dinner.'

Charlotte did her best to hide the apprehension she felt at the mere idea of getting on Filinha's back again. 'Wonderful, I'm starving. How long will they take?'

'Not long, greedy one. While they cook I shall unsaddle the horses and gather more wood, so we may be warm.' He smiled at her reassuringly and strode off, his spurs jangling. Charlotte stared after him thoughtfully, then concentrated resolutely on the sunset, which was spectacular enough to demand her full attention, diverting her from thoughts of the journey back. She watched in awe as the bright gold of sunset turned slowly to a glowing orange, then deepened to crimson and purple, like a great multicoloured veil some giant hand was pulling down the edge of the world to reveal the huge, brilliant stars that appeared, cluster by cluster in its wake. She shivered as the light faded, wondering how they would find their way in the dark, bitterly regretting her earlier obstinacy about turning back. She crouched forlornly close to the flames, her mouth watering as the sizzling hunks of beef began to give out a tantalising aroma.

'You feel better?' asked Roberto, returning with an armful of branches. He looked at her sharply as he augmented the blaze. 'You are aching badly, *não é*?'

She nodded glumly, her teeth caught in her lower lip, and Roberto turned to her and took her hands.

'Charlotte, we have made camp here because I could see that you were unable to ride any farther.'

'What?' She looked about her wildly. 'You mean we're going to stay here all night?'

'Do not be angry. Please!' His grasp tightened. 'We have made poorer time than I intended. We could not have reached Estancia Velha before dark, even if you had been able to ride that far tonight. So we shall eat this good beef, and eat the bread Valdemar gave me, and then we shall talk for a while and drink *café*, and then you will go to sleep.'

'On what?' she demanded.

'We shall use the blankets from our horses, Charlotte.' He bent closer, his eyes urgent. 'Do not be frightened, *querida*. At first light we shall ride again.'

Charlotte swallowed hard. 'I'm not frightened exactly, Roberto. I just need time to get used to the idea, that's all.' She breathed in deeply, and managed a smile. 'Just think what a tale I'll have to tell William when I get home!'

Roberto touched her cheek gently, his eyes eloquent with admiration. 'You are a brave girl. Charlotte. Believe me when I say that spending the night out here in the *campo* was not my intention.'

He turned away to attend to the meat, and Charlotte watched, fascinated, as he turned the meat skilfully with the point of the knife he had taken from the ornate silver sheath hanging from his belt.

'If seduction were on your mind there must be easier ways of stage-managing it. And more comfortable locations for it, too,' she added with a chuckle. Roberto's answering laugh held relief.

'*E verdade*, Charlotte!' He looked at her very directly across the flames, which shone brighter as the sky grew dark. 'I will never try to seduce you, Charlotte, you have my word. Your virginity is a gift you must be free to bestow on the man fortunate enough to be your husband.'

She gazed at him, lips parted. 'I believe you really mean than, Roberto!'

'Be very sure that I do.' He took a smaller knife from a pocket in the pleated *bombachas*. 'And now I shall show you how to eat your *churrasco*. The meat is ready, I think.'

'Please say it is,' said Charlotte with fervour. 'I don't think I can last out much longer.'

'*Calma!*' He laughed and sliced off a piece of meat with the larger knife, impaled it on the smaller one and handed the latter to her with a bow. 'Try that, *carinha*.'

The meat was red hot, slightly charred on the outside and quite the most wonderful delicacy Charlotte had ever eaten. She chewed ecstatically, accepting the hunk of bread he gave her before he sliced off a helping of meat for himself. Roberto set the coffee-pot on the embers, then sat down beside Charlotte, laughing delightedly at her relish for the primitive meal.

'Lord, if my mother could see me now!' said Charlotte indistinctly. 'No plates, no forks, no napkins, and never a speck of sauce in sight, just meat, wonderful meat, and me squatting on the ground to eat it.'

Roberto sliced off another morsel for her. 'Your mother would not care for our *churrasco*?'

'A bit basic for *Maman*. She takes food very seriously.' Charlotte grinned cheerfully as she shifted her aching legs with caution. 'Dad, now, would revel in all this. Just his sort of thing.'

Roberto ate in silence for a while, his eyes on the flames. 'Your parents would not be pleased to know you were alone here with me like this, I think, Charlotte.'

She held out her knife for more meat. 'Probably not, but they don't know, Roberto, so let's not think of that. Besides, *Maman* is very practical. If she finds a situation unavoidable she makes the best of it—so I shall do the same.' She grinned at him cheerfully, 'And I certainly can't fault the food, it's heavenly!'

Roberto provided her with another sizzling morsel. 'I regret that the accommodation is less pleasing!'

'Oh, I don't know.' She waved a hand at the spangled indigo sky. 'The decor at this hotel is out of this world—shame the bed's so hard!'

Roberto laughed with her, then turned his attention to the last of the meat, sharing it out between them.

'Roberto,' said Charlotte, 'will you tell me about your wife?'

Roberto's face went blank. 'Why do you wish to talk about Amalha?'

'I imagine it's a fair time until dawn. We must talk about something.'

'We shall sleep between now and dawn, I trust!'

'But in the meantime you tell me about Amalha and I'll tell you anything you want to know about the men in my life,' coaxed Charlotte.

Roberto shrugged. 'Very well, but the lady must be first. You shall begin.'

So while they drank the coffee-pot dry Charlotte told Roberto about Alan Bragg, and several other young men who took her to theatres and cinemas, even to the occasional nightclub, or just out for a drive and a meal.

'And, of course, there's Ben Ackroyd,' said Charlotte gloomily as Roberto replenished the fire. The outline of his profile hardened like beaten copper against the light from the new flames.

'He is the man your father wants for you?' he asked quietly.

'It would be very convenient, certainly. He's Dad's general manager and a clever business man, and—well, I don't think he's at all averse to the idea of marrying me.'

'That is not difficult to believe.' Roberto sat a little farther away when he returned to the rug.

Charlotte shook her head. 'I meant he's keen to marry the the boss's daughter, that's all. Ben's ambitious. I'm not sure he'd fancy me so much if my name weren't Mercer.'

'Then he is a fool!' Roberto eyed her sombrely. 'You are everything any man could desire, Charlotte.'

'Even without my money?'

'*Sem duvida.*' He shrugged in disbelief. 'Do you truthfully not know how beautiful you are?'

Charlotte looked away, colouring. 'Even with a grubby face and creaking bones?'

'Even so,' he said matter-of-factly. 'But do not marry this Ackroyd man just because it is convenient, Charlotte. A marriage without love is not something I would recommend, from bitter experience.'

'Why did you marry Amalha, then, if you didn't care for her?'

Roberto stretched out, his head propped against his saddle, his eyes absent as he gazed into the flames. 'Ildefonso Braga was ill, and wanted his only unmarried daughter settled before he died. He and my father were friends. They arranged the marriage between them.' He looked at Charlotte with a sardonic smile. 'This must seem strange to you, *carinha*. And nowadays such marriages are rarer here, but ten years ago, when Amalha and I were both so young, it was not unusual, particularly with the children of two friends. Amalha was very beautiful, dark and vivid, but wilful. She was born late to Ildefonso, and allowed to run wild, to ride all day with the men, sometimes for days and nights at a time. Old Ildefonso was glad, I think, to get her off his hands. So. We were married. And only then did I learn that the physical side of love was nothing new to her. Compared with her I was the merest novice and she taunted me with it, told

me she had a lover, one of the men she rode herd
with at home. She was running away to meet him
the day...' He breathed in deeply. 'It is why I did
not go to look for her. He must have grown tired
of waiting, assumed Amalha had changed her mind,
because he went away without her. And so she died
alone out here in the *campo*.'

Charlotte shivered, her eyes on the great fiery
clusters of stars. 'Was it dark like this?'

'No. She ran from me at first light, and I cursed
her and let her go and went off with the others as
usual. It was not the first time Amalha had ridden
off in a rage. Her horse came back without her, so
my father took some men to search for her. You
know the rest.'

Charlotte moved close to Roberto and touched
his arm very gently. 'I'm sorry. Don't talk about it
any more.'

'Perhaps it is good that I do.' Roberto's hand
covered hers. 'It was so terrible, Charlotte, because
I did not love Amalha, nor even like her very much.
I think she liked my father far more than me.' His
mouth twisted. 'God knows he was kinder to her.'

'Let's talk about something else,' said Charlotte
firmly. 'I'm sorry I ever mentioned the subject.'

'Shall we discuss your aches and pains?' He sat
upright to smile at her.

'That makes me sound like an arthritic old
crone!'

Roberto cast his eyes heavenwards. 'Would that
you were. Our present situation would be very much
easier for me if this were so!'

Charlotte smiled with saccharine innocence.
'Really? Why?'

'Because, Miss Charlotte Mercer, since you are a woman of intelligence, you know well that for any man to spend a night alone with you, out here where there is no other soul even near, is a situation fraught with temptation, however uncomfortable the conditions.' He laid a hand on his heart. 'But I have promised that your virtue is safe with me, and——'

'You never break a promise!' she finished for him, then yawned suddenly, surprised to realise she was tired.

Roberto sprang to his feet at once. '*Sonolenta*— little sleepy head! I shall prepare your couch this instant, *Dona Carlota*.'

Charlotte got up awkwardly, gritting her teeth as her aching muscles protested. 'It's been a wonderful day, Roberto. Thank you so much for bringing me.'

Roberto laid two sheepskins on the ground a short distance from the fire, covered them with the blankets, and rolled his jerkin into a pillow on one of the makeshift beds. 'Yours, Charlotte. I shall sleep a discreet distance away—and keep that distance. Have no fear.'

Charlotte had no fear of any kind, she found; not of Roberto, nor of the impenetrable darkness beyond their fire, not even of her isolation from any form of habitation. She took off the boots, put on her windbreaker, rolled herself in the blanket and lay down on the sheepskin, wrinkling her nose at the strong smell of horse. She curled herself gingerly into a ball and burrowed her head into the warmth of Roberto's jerkin. 'I'll be fine,' she assured him drowsily. 'Can you manage without a pillow?'

'I have survived in the open with less sophisticated comforts than these!' Roberto dropped on one knee beside her, his eyes tender as he put a hand on her hair, running his fingers gently down the length of the braid. '*Dorme bem, carinha*. Sleep well.' He bent lower and dropped a kiss on the crown of her head, then sprang up and retired to his own blanket. Charlotte lay with her back towards him, her eyes heavy with sleep as she listened to the clink of his spurs as he removed his boots. There was a crackle as he added more wood to the fire, and the faint movements of his settling in, and she drifted off to sleep with the sound of his whispered '*Boa noite*, Charlotte,' in her ears.

It was still dark when Charlotte woke in such discomfort that she gasped in pain, and at once Robert was kneeling by her side. He struck a match to see her face, demanding to know what was wrong.

'I feel as if someone's tied all my muscles into knots—very fancy ones! And I'm cold.' She tried to get up and groaned, and Roberto cursed softly and pulled her gently to a sitting position, exclaiming as he felt her hands.

'They are like icicles, *carinha*.' In his anxiety he chafed them until they hurt and she protested feebly.

'Steady on! I'll need them to ride in the morning—ow!' She let out another yelp as pain shot through her when she tried to move.

'Lie face down,' ordered Roberto and moved to blow on the ashes of the fire, adding more wood as the embers glowed into life.

Awkwardly Charlotte did as he said, groaning as she spreadeagled herself on the sheepskin. She heard a whicker as the horses moved uneasily at the sound of their voices, and Roberto went quickly to quiet the animals, then returned to drop on his knees alongside her.

'I am going to try to loosen those muscles of yours, Charlotte,' he said briskly. 'So relax, *carinha*, do not tense against me. It will hurt at first.'

He was right. Charlotte's teeth clenched, sweat pearling her forehead despite the cold, as Roberto's strong, hard fingers found the knotted muscles of her back and shoulders and worked to release their tension. After an agonising interval the pain began to lessen as the muscles relaxed and she let out an unsteady sigh of relief.

'Better?' he asked tersely, and she waggled an outstretched hand at him.

'M'm. Much better.' She screwed her head round to look at him. 'Why have you stopped?'

He cleared his throat. 'Shall I move lower, Charlotte?'

Charlotte shrugged impatiently, happy to find she could do so without hurting. 'For heaven's sake, Roberto. Do get on with it!'

Still he hesitated. 'Charlotte, it would be of no use to massage you through your jeans——'

'Then I'll take them off,' she said promptly. 'Or, easier still,' she fumbled beneath her midriff, 'I'll undo the zip and you pull them off.'

In silence he did as she said, and Charlotte waited expectantly, but nothing happened. She turned her head to see him staring down at her long, tanned legs, his mouth compressed, then he breathed deeply and began his ministrations on the back of her hips, through the cotton of her shirt and briefs, and for a while she closed her eyes in blessed relief as the aching lessened. Then his hands reached the smooth skin at the top of her thighs and everything changed. Charlotte came alive to problems other than aching muscles. Now she had nerve-ends which flared into life at the touch of Roberto's hands. He faltered for a moment in his kneading and probing, and Charlotte bit her lip, trying to relax, clamping down on the need to gasp and moan under his touch, fighting the urge to roll over on her back and hold up her arms to him.

With a choked sound Roberto sprang to his feet and turned his back, and Charlotte scrambled back into her jeans in ungraceful haste, zipping them with hands that shook. She buckled her belt, and looked up at Roberto's broad-shouldered silhouette, outlined against the firelight.

'Thank you,' she said huskily. 'I feel very much better.'

'*Parabems*—congratulations. I do not.' Viciously he kicked one of the logs deeper into the fire.

'Roberto...' Charlotte trailed into silence as he turned on her, standing with legs apart, his hands on his narrow hips as he glared down at her.

'Go to sleep, Charlotte!' He threw himself down on his own sheepskin, turning his back as he tugged the blanket round his shoulders.

She stared forlornly at him, then with a sigh pulled her own blanket round her, feeling cold. There was a long, uneasy silence, while both of them lay motionless, each of them conscious of the other's wakefulness. After a while Charlotte's teeth began to chatter, and with a despairing groan Roberto jumped to his feet, dragged his sheepskin close to hers and plucked the blanket away from her shivering body. Without a word he lay down beside her, turning her away from him to hold her cradled in the curve of his body as he secured both blankets over them and settled his head next to hers on the jerkin.

'Say nothing, Charlotte,' he said, his tone so autocratic she obeyed meekly. 'Do not move. Not even an eyelash. Thus we shall contrive to pass the night in some kind of comfort—for you at least.'

Charlotte lay motionless, warm at last with her back against Roberto's hard, protective body, hardly daring to breathe. Something in his voice persuaded her to do as he said without question, and she stared hopelessly into the darkness, wondering how he expected her to sleep under the circumstances. Nevertheless, after a while, since she had ordered it to keep so utterly still, her body assumed she meant it to sleep, and her eyelids drooped, her breathing grew deeper, and the next thing she knew it was daylight and she was the sole occupant of her sheepskin couch.

'Roberto!' she cried, struggling to her feet in a panic, then relief flooded through her as she saw him emerge from the trees. He ran towards her, pulling on his shirt.

'Charlotte? What is it?'

She threw herself into his arms. 'I didn't know where you were.' She rubbed her face against his bare chest, feeling the quick thudding of his heart against her cheek. His arms crushed her to him and blissfully she breathed in the smell of man and horse and security and raised her head to see his eyes blazing down at her. *'Bom dia, Senhor Monteiro,'* she whispered. 'How are you today?'

'Querida!' He groaned and bent his head, kissing her with a desperation that told her he was at the end of his tether. 'I can bear no more,' he muttered between kisses. 'After the night I have spent I have no defence against you, Charlotte.' His mouth took hers again and her lips parted and their tongues met and his hands pressed against her hips, moulding her to him as hers slid round his neck to hold him as close as she could. When they finally broke apart they were both breathing in great gasps, staring at each other in something very like anguish.

Roberto pulled himself together with such palpable effort Charlotte was shaken by a surge of love for him as he buttoned his shirt with fingers that shook.

'Charlotte——' he began, and fell silent, unable to find words to express his feelings.

Her eyes dropped and she pulled the elastic band from the end of her braid and began unravelling her hair with fingers even less steady than Roberto's. 'A good thing you didn't kiss me last night,' she said breathlessly.

'A *good* thing?' he echoed. 'A miraculous thing, Miss Mercer. I am full of admiration for myself. I shall be known as São Roberto the Pure from this day on! Could you not tell how much I wanted—

burned to turn you round in my arms and kiss you senseless? But, saint that I am, I did not, because——'

'You gave me your word!' she finished for him and laughed at him and he laughed with her, fingering the dark stubble on his chin as he scrutinised the tell-tale redness on her chin.

'I have scratched you, *carinha*. I apologise.'

'I didn't even notice,' she assured him, and swung away to make for the stream. 'And now I shall wash my face and prepare to——' She whirled round again, smiling radiantly. 'Roberto! I'm hardly aching at all! What a miracle worker you are!'

He bowed modestly. 'As I said—*São Roberto, sempre as seus ordems, senhora.*'

Charlotte giggled and went off to splash cold water on her face at the stream while Roberto saddled the horses. As she braided her hair again her stomach gave a sudden rumble and she sighed, wishing there was something to eat, but almost certain everything had been polished off the night before. She hurried back to Roberto as fast as she could, driven again by the feeling she had experienced first in Prestleigh; a disturbing reluctance to be parted from him an instant longer than necessary. She pushed the thought from her mind. Until she left Brazil she would live for the moment, she decided, and gave Roberto a smile of such brilliance as she reached him he pretended to reel, and hand in front of his eyes.

'You dazzle me, Charlotte.'

'I bet you say that to all the *senhoritas*!'

'You have my word I do not. For one thing I do not know another *senhorita* by the name of

Charlotte!' He laughed and dodged as she aimed a playful fist at him. 'Do not hurt me, *carinha*, I implore—besides,' he added smugly. 'If you hit me I shall not give you the treat I have saved for this morning.'

Charlotte's eyes lit with hope. 'Bread? Coffee?'

Roberto dived into the extra saddlebag and produced two big oranges with triumph. 'What will you give me for one of these, my so beautiful Miss Mercer?'

'What do you want?'

'One kiss. A modest request.' His eyes gleamed and she shook her head at him reprovingly.

'You are not a gentleman, Senhor Monteiro.'

He shrugged, impenitent. '*E verdade*. I am just a man.'

Charlotte eyed the orange he held out of reach above her head, then cast down her eyelashes and peeped at him through them. 'Very well. Take your kiss, then.'

'*Sim, senhora,*' he said with alacrity, and threw the oranges down on the grass so that he could pull her into his arms, looking down at her for an instant. 'Is it such a sacrifice, *querida*?'

'No.' Her eyes were lambent with candour. 'I want you to kiss me. I wanted you to last night.'

'I had promised——'

'To respect my fabled virtue—I know, I know! But I don't see what harm a kiss or two would have done.'

'Do you not, Charlotte?' He drew her closer. 'Alone in the dark, together under the blankets, do you really not know what harm one solitary kiss would have done?' His mouth curved in a smile which brought the blood rushing to her newly washed cheeks. 'Then perhaps I should show you once more, *querida*.' He bent and took her mouth with his, parting her lips with his tongue, tasting her, caressing her, one hand moving to cup her breast, to open her shirt and smooth away the minimum protection afforded by her fragile lace bra. Charlotte gasped as he moved his head down, clutching his back convulsively as his lips closed on a hardening peak. His tongue flicked and his teeth grazed and she let out a choked, harsh cry and he pulled her down on the dewy grass and hauled her close along his entire length while his mouth returned to hers and his fingers stroked and teased her breasts until she shook with longing. The waves of sensation radiated to every part of her, starting up a hungry ache deep within her body. She arched against him mindlessly, her fingers scrabbling at his shirt buttons, desperate to thrust her bare flesh against his chest. With an agonised sound Roberto thrust her away and jumped to his feet, bending to pull her up. He took her by the elbows and shook her slightly, staring hotly into her dazed eyes.

'Now you see why one kiss is spark enough to result in a complete conflagration!'

'I do now.' She shrugged helplessly. 'I've been kissed a lot, but I've never felt anything remotely like—like that.'

The tension drained slowly from Roberto's face. 'Have you not, *cara*? I am glad. I too have never experienced such desperation to possess.'

She sighed, and turned away to put herself together again.

'Forgive me, Charlotte,' he said. 'I did not mean to frighten you.'

'You didn't.' She tucked her shirt firmly in her jeans. 'At least not in one way. It was frightening to learn how easily the whole thing can happen, after all. I've never before understood how women don't call a halt when things get out of hand.' She turned to face him. 'Because I'd never lost a shred of control in such situations before, I assumed I never would. Naïve, wasn't I?'

Roberto stroked his chin pensively. 'Could it be that because for you and me there is something more than the base desire to couple? That perhaps we have an affinity you have not found with other men? I, most certainly, have never experienced quite that same sense of utter rightness in a woman's arms.'

'Chemistry, most people call it, Roberto.' She bent to pick up one of the fallen oranges. 'Whatever it is makes one hungry. May I have my breakfast now?'

He laughed. 'Not only may you have your breakfast, *carinha*, but I shall peel it for you.'

Shortly afterwards they were mounted and on their way again, their progress still slow, because Charlotte's muscles, though infinitely better than she would ever have believed possible at one stage, still protested if put to any great exertion. As a result it was almost noon before they came in sight of the eucalyptus trees shading Roberto's little house. As they drew near Charlotte saw the jeep standing near by, and Roberto sighed heavily.

She looked at him quickly. 'What is it? Visitors?'

'In a way.' He gave her a very odd, sidelong smile. 'The *Patrão* has come to welcome us home, it seems.' He swung out of the saddle and tethered the horses, then held up his arms to Charlotte. She slid down into them and he held her tightly for a moment before setting her on her feet. As they went towards the house a man appeared on the veranda, watching them as they approached. He was elegant, in a light tweed jacket and immaculate riding breeches, his glossy boots a far cry from the dusty wrinkled affairs Roberto was wearing. Charlotte's eyes narrowed as she realised that if this stranger's clothes were different from Roberto's, his features were quite definitely not. His close-curling hair was threaded with grey, and there were a few lines on his aquiline face, but otherwise the *Patrão* and Roberto Monteiro were so alike it was obvious to anyone with half an eye that they were related. She turned stricken eyes on Roberto's set, unsmiling face, then lifted her chin proudly as the slim, handsome man came down the shallow steps to greet her.

'At last we meet, Miss Mercer.' His voice was husky, like Roberto's, the accent more pronounced. He held out his hand. 'Let me assure you that it was Roberto's choice, not mine, to wait so long for our introduction. However, since your overnight absence has given cause for much anxiety I decided to disobey my son and came to await your return in person. I am Luis Roberto Monteiro, and I am enchanted to make your acquaintance.'

Charlotte summoned a smile and gave him her hand, her mind in turmoil. 'How do you do, Senhor

Monteiro. I'm deeply sorry to have caused you any distress.'

Luis Monteiro smiled and kissed her hand gracefully. 'Since you were not aware of my existence, due to this little *comédia* of Roberto's, I absolve you of all blame.' The black eyes hardened as they rested on his son. 'You, however, *meu filho*, are required to give me an explanation, *não é*? What in the name of God can you have been thinking of to keep this young lady out all night when she is a visitor at our home, and therefore under our protection?'

CHAPTER NINE

'Charlotte needs rest. I shall accompany you to the house and account to you there, *Pai*, if you will be so good as to wait.' Roberto turned to Charlotte, his lips bleak as they met the look in hers. 'There is much explanation necessary, I know, Charlotte.'

She raised a quizzical eyebrow. 'I look forward to it.'

Luis Monteiro looked from one taut face to the other with unashamed interest. 'I trust you will do us the honour of dining with us at the house this evening, Miss Mercer,' he suggested blandly. 'Until eight, my dear. *Até ja.*'

Charlotte inclined her head regally and turned on her booted, spurred heel and marched into the house, ignoring Roberto. Teresa rushed to her at once, exclaiming over her and clucking like a mother hen as she ran a bath full of hot water, promising food as soon as Dona Carlota was dressed. Wearily Charlotte stripped off her dusty clothes and sank into the water, the comfort of it so potent it eased just a little the angry pain she felt at Roberto's deception.

How he must have laughed at her, she thought, eyes kindling as she looked round her at the tiny, stark bathroom and wondered who was the actual owner. Of course it must belong to the Monteiros, but who actually lived in it? All that rubbish about gauchos and the liberty of the spirit! Charlotte soaped herself angrily. And all the time Roberto was the son of the *Patrão*—what a blockhead she had been. But why had he felt it necessary to play the simple cow-hand? What motive could he have had for keeping her in the dark? Charlotte gave a frustrated moan as she remembered the cheque hurled at him with such patronising scorn. To the heir apparent of Estancia Velha the money for the Presteigne estate must have seemed quite a joke. She blew out her cheeks explosively and reached for her shampoo. Tonight she must look her best. As formal as possible, too. She was grateful now that her mother had insisted she include at least one pretty dress in her luggage. She would show these Monteiros that a sensible Yorkshire lass had no problems with how to behave in a formal Brazilian household. Perhaps Roberto had been ashamed to take her to his father's house, afraid she might not know which knife and fork to use at the dinner-table! Charlotte's eyes flashed as she wrapped herself in a towel and went in search of pyjamas and dressing-gown, her hair swathed turbanwise in a towel. First she needed food, then a good sleep so that by tonight she would look her best; bright-eyed, glossy-haired, a match for any man, Roberto Monteiro included.

The food was the easy part. Teresa had scrambled eggs and grilled smoked bacon very crisply, and there was a jug of fruit juice and a great pot of coffee alongside a miniature mountain of toast. Charlotte smiled gratefully at the hovering girl and began to demolish the lot, assuring Teresa as best she could that she was unharmed by her adventure in the *campo*.

Afterwards, in the small darkened bedroom, sleep was harder to achieve. The memories of the night were too fresh, too disturbing to let her rest. Her mind kept going over the moments in the darkness on the hard ground, safe and warm in Roberto's close embrace, and the softer bed of the present became uncomfortable as she tossed and turned on it, restless at the thought of Roberto's kisses, of his hands... She buried her head in the pillow, forcing her body to lie still, willing her mind to stay blank. Concentrate on his duplicity, she commanded herself. Never mind the kisses, remember the deceit.

Eventually Charlotte slept so heavily she neither heard the jeep arrive, nor the hushed voices outside the house. When she woke it was late, and she got up yawning to go in search of coffee before she began to dress. As Teresa provided it she told Charlotte Senhor Roberto had been while she slept. Charlotte thanked her thoughtfully. So he had come to apologise, had he? We'll see about that, she thought. If he wanted to see her he could wait until tonight in his own house, instead of sneaking back here to visit her, like some married man with a mistress tucked conveniently away.

Before her nap Charlotte had braided her hair in numbers of plaits and curled up the ends with strips of wide silk ribbon she used for special occasions. The result was gratifying. When it was brushed out her hair hung down on her shoulders in a shower of ripples, the ends curling against her tanned shoulders exactly as she wanted it. Her face was browner after her long ride in the sun, but with a generous application of moisturiser, a skilful touch of blusher and eyeshadow her reflection glowed, burnished, from the mirror. She added bronze-red lipstick, flicked brown mascara on her lashes and stood, eyeing herself objectively. The transformation from travel-stained scruff to elegant dinner-guest was almost complete. And the dress Janine Mercer had packed for her daughter with such exquisite care was as feminine and pretty as any of her own. For once Charlotte had yielded to persuasion and chosen bias-cut chiffon: ankle-length, black, and printed here and there with bronze and white chrysanthemums. The dress was strapless, with its own huge scarf for a wrap, and as Charlotte smoothed the clinging skirt into place she gave her reflection a quick nod of approval. No necklace to break the expanse of smooth tanned skin, just two gold hoops in her ears, two gilt barrettes to hold her hair away from her face, plain black satin pumps, small black satin purse, and Charlotte Mercer was ready to take on the world.

'*Senhora! Jorge Pires espera no carro,*' called Teresa, and Charlotte scowled as she swathed herself in the chiffon wrap, not at all pleased to learn that Roberto had sent someone else to fetch her.

Head high, she sailed from her room, and Teresa clapped her hands together in admiration at the sight of her.

'*Que linda, Dona Carlota,*' she said fervently. '*Muita chique!*'

Charlotte thanked her and went outside to find Jorge Pires waiting beside the bonnet of a large black Mercedes. He bowed, greeting her courteously as he opened the car door for her, and

Charlotte bade him a pleasant good evening, waved at Teresa and leaned back in the car's comfortable leather-scented interior, trying to quell the butterflies fluttering in her middle region.

When Jorge Pires brought the car to a halt it was exactly eight by the clock on the dashboard, and Charlotte gave the Brazilian her hand as he helped her to alight, her eyebrows rising as she looked at the main house at Estancia Velha for the first time. Her glimpse from the air had been no preparation for the grace and grandeur of the colonial-style building. A flight of steps led to a colonnaded veranda with pillars worthy of the façade of Covent Garden Opera House. White-painted shutters flanked doors and windows on both floors of the two-storey house, which, with its pale walls and red roof set against a crescent of sheltering trees, gave the impression of a painting in a frame.

As Charlotte started up the steps two figures emerged from the house and stood waiting to welcome her. Backlit by the houselights in the darkness and dressed in identical white dinner jackets, the two men could have been brothers until Charlotte was near enough to hold out her hand to Luis Monteiro, whose greying hair distinguished him from his son. So did his gleaming smile of welcome, as he raised her hand to his lips and kissed it.

'*Boa tarde*, Miss Mercer. You are punctual. Welcome to Estancia Velha.'

'Thank you, Senhor Monteiro.' Charlotte smiled at him warmly, then turned to extend her hand to Roberto, whose face wore a guarded expression as he bent over her fingers and touched his lips to them fleetingly. He drew back instantly, his mouth tight, and Charlotte smiled at him serenely to hide the leap of blood in her veins at his touch. 'Good evening, Roberto.'

He inclined his head gravely. 'Charlotte. I trust you have recovered from your ride.'

'Oh, yes. I had a bath, a huge breakfast and a long, peaceful sleep and now I'm right as rain,' she said airily.

Luis Monteiro took her arm and led her into the house, directly into a big imposing room with white walls and gleaming wood floors scattered with rugs glowing in the muted colours of old Persia. The furniture varied from Louis the Fifteenth gilt chairs to brass-studded hide sofas, two of which flanked a great stone fireplace at one end of the room. A huge oil-painting of horsemen and cattle hung above it. There were several similar scenes on the other walls, all the pictures in heavy gilded frames. Nothing, it seemed to Charlotte at first glance, was on a small scale in the Monteiro household, from the great copper pots of flowers standing on massive carved chests to the porcelain lamps which glowed at various points around the room.

'How beautiful,' said Charlotte, impressed.

'I am glad you like it.' Luis Monteiro waved her to a sofa upholstered in dull rose brocade, and at once a dark young woman appeared with a heavy silver tray of drinks and set it down near the *Patrão*. 'For some ladies' taste the room is a little——' he spread his hands, searching for the word.

'Overpowering?' suggested Charlotte.

'*Exactamente!* Sometimes my English deserts me. Since my Laura died I do not speak it so much as

I should.' Luis glanced at his son. 'Roberto. Give our guest a champagne cocktail, *por favor*.'

Roberto glanced at Charlotte. 'Is that to your taste? If not we have most other things.'

'It sounds wonderful.' Charlotte accepted a frosty, fragile goblet from him with a polite smile and sipped its contents. 'M'm. It tastes wonderful, too. Thank you.'

Roberto seated himself a short distance away, listening intently as Charlotte replied to his father's questions about her impressions of his country, in particular of Estancia Velha.

'It's utterly breathtaking. Of course some of my first impressions were a little mistaken,' she added delicately, and smiled at Roberto, whose stillness had the air of a tiger poised for the kill. 'For some reason, Senhor Monteiro, your son decided to play a practical joke on me about his identity. His disguise was quite perfect—so colourful. I really must take a photograph of him in his, er, working-clothes before I leave.' From the corner of her eye she saw Roberto's face darken, and he drained his glass suddenly.

Luis de Monteiro laughed and lifted a finger to his son, who refilled Charlotte's glass and then his father's without a word. 'Roberto has explained his reasons to me, Miss Mercer. And while I did not approve, I could not forbid, you understand. Roberto is too old for that.' The aristocratic face took on a formidable expression. 'Nevertheless, when I was informed that you had not returned last night I was—was——'

'Outraged,' supplied Roberto evenly.

His father nodded. '*Isso!* A young English lady in our care is kept out all night in the *campo* and I should be calm?' The black Monteiro eyes flashed. '*Deus me livre!* I am only grateful the child came to no harm.'

Roberto's chin lifted angrily. 'You knew she would not. She was with me.'

Luis tapped his nose pensively. '*E verdade.* It was a thought both reassuring and disturbing.'

'Oh, your son took every care of me,' Charlotte felt obliged to point out. 'He wanted me to turn back much earlier, you know, but I was enjoying myself so much I persuaded him to let me go a little farther with the others.' She smiled ruefully. 'I never dreamed my muscles would give out on me the way they did.'

Luis cast a whimsical glance at his son. 'One thing I understand most perfectly, Roberto. If Miss Mercer used persuasion, it is easy to see how impossible it was to refuse her.'

'I was a fool to allow her to ride so far,' said Roberto shortly, and rose to offer Charlotte another drink.

She refused prettily. 'I think not. Delicious but potent. Any more and I might use the wrong knife and fork.'

Luis laughed. 'I hope your dinner tonight will be an improvement on the one you ate last night, Charlotte. I have permission to call you Charlotte?'

'Please do.' Charlotte was beginning to feel warm under the unwavering scrutiny of Roberto's black eyes, but kept her wrap swathed securely round her shoulders, wishing now she had worn something else. When the maid came to say dinner was ready

Luis led the way through double doors into a formal dining-room where a rosewood table gleamed with delicate crystal and china by the light of candles in heavy silver holders. The chairs were intricately carved and inset with wicker, and swagged, draped curtains in straw-coloured satin hung at the windows. It was all, thought Charlotte coldly, a far cry from the modest little house Roberto had lodged her in for her stay. She looked up at him questioningly as he held her chair for her, and glimpsed a flame of response for an instant before he moved away to seat himself opposite, while Luis Monteiro took his place at the head of the table.

Unable to eat while swathed in folds of chiffon, Charlotte had no choice but to remove her wrap and let it hang over the back of her chair. There was an odd silence, and she looked up to see both men gazing at her, Luis with mingled admiration and amusement, Roberto's eyes molten with an expression Charlotte recognised with triumph. He wanted her, and had trouble in concealing the fact. In the great mirror hanging on the wall behind him she caught a glimpse of herself. Candlelight played on the satin-smooth skin of her shoulders, emphasising the shadow between her breasts above the chiffon, and she exulted in the fact that she had never looked better in her life.

'It is a great pleasure to entertain so beautiful a guest,' said Luis, and motioned to the maid to fill the wine-glasses, while a second girl served them with crisp lettuce hearts stuffed with giant prawns in a dressing Charlotte tasted with appreciation.

'Exquisite! My mother would love this—can you tell me how the sauce is made?' she asked Roberto,

who stared at her blankly for a moment, as though
she spoke in an unknown language.

'I—I am not sure.' He turned to the maid.
'Figenia—o molho. Tem conhaque?'

'Sim, senhor. E creme de leite.'

'Brandy and cream added to the cook's special
mayonnaise,' said Roberto, and Charlotte smiled
her thanks, after which it fell to Luis Monteiro to
keep the conversation flowing during the meal, as
he questioned Charlotte with interest about her
family and life in Prestleigh.

'Such beautiful hair,' he remarked at one point.
'The colour—it is like your father?'

Charlotte shook back the bright ripples, smiling.
'Yes, but not quite as fiery as his, thank heavens.
I'm a mixture of both my parents, so is William—
but he's luckier than me. He's got Dad's blue eyes
and *Maman*'s dark hair.'

'Ah yes, I remember your so charming mother.
A very beautiful lady, with eyes just like yours,
Charlotte,' said Luis, smiling lazily as Roberto shot
him a very unfilial look.

Charlotte changed the subject hurriedly, asking
if the *Patrão* also rode with the herd as she had
done.

'My father has an injured leg,' said Roberto. 'It
does not allow him the activity he would prefer.'

'It is true,' said Luis, sighing. 'The title *"Patrão"*
is no longer mine, by right. It is Roberto who runs
Estancia Velha these days.'

Roberto smiled warmly for the first time. *'Não
importa, Pai.* You will always be the *Patrão.'*

'Until the moment I breathe my last, when Roberto will be *Patrão*,' Luis told Charlotte, shrugging philosophically.

'Very dynastic,' she said, impressed.

'But alas I have no other sons to help him.' Luis shot a wry look at Roberto's wooden face. 'If I had, perhaps I might have grandsons by now.'

'You should have married again,' said Roberto curtly.

Luis Monteiro's distinguished face shadowed. 'No. My Laura was the only woman for me.' He smiled at Charlotte. 'It does not do to love one woman so much that when she dies she takes a man's heart with her to the grave.'

Charlotte's eyes were warm with sympathy. 'You must have loved your wife very much, Senhor Monteiro.'

'Ah yes. We loved—and fought and then loved again.' Luis cast an eye at his son's face. 'But I think I embarrass my son. You have only the one brother, Charlotte?'

She smiled. 'Just the one, but he's only four years old. My father had to wait a very long time for him, so in the meantime he tried his best to make a son out of me.'

'*Meu Deus!*' Luis laughed. 'I do not think he succeeded.'

'Do not be deceived by Charlotte's looks,' said Roberto. 'She is an efficient businesswoman who runs her father's property affairs very successfully in his absence.'

Luis leaned to fill Charlotte's wine-glass. 'And is that what you want of life, Charlotte?'

She hesitated. 'My life is full, and challenging, and most of the time I enjoy it, but as I've told Roberto, I always wanted to paint.' She smiled at them both. 'Perhaps I shall one day, now Father has William and I'm not as essential to the plan as I used to be.' Her smile deepened. 'Though heaven knows what will happen if William wants to paint too—or drive a truck or be a ballet dancer. I just hope I'm a long, long way from the explosion if he does!'

'It is natural to want a son to carry on the family tradition.' Luis looked at his son with affection. 'Roberto is as good a cow-hand as any on Estancia Velha, and has also the brain for the administration. I consider myself very fortunate, yet I grieve that he has no son yet to follow him. It is time that he begins his family.'

Roberto got up abruptly and stalked round the table to hold Charlotte's chair for her. 'Now, however, is the time to ply our guest with coffee and our excellent local brandy before I drive her back. She must be tired.'

'She does not look in the least tired!' Luis Monteiro's eyes rested on his guest with overt pleasure. 'Such radiance lights up our home, Charlotte.'

She thanked him warmly, but this time let Roberto escort her back to the great *sala*, where he seated her before a heavy silver coffee-service. For the rest of the evening, as Charlotte poured coffee and tasted the brandy, Robert steered the conversation adroitly to anecdotes of life on Estancia Velha, and half an hour later Charlotte rose to go, thanking her host gracefully.

Luis Monteiro held her hand in his as he wished her goodnight. 'It is strange to you perhaps, Charlotte, to be obliged to stay in that little house, but here in the *casa* we are two men alone. It would not be proper for you to stay here.' He raised her hand to his and kissed it. 'Goodnight, *carinha*. Sleep well.'

The silence was tangible in the Mercedes as Roberto drove the short distance to the little house, which was in darkness except for a light burning in the living-room.

'Teresa must be in bed,' said Charlotte, and held out her hand as they reached the veranda. 'I'll say goodnight, then.'

Roberto took her hand in his and held it fast. 'Please allow me to come in, Charlotte. I will stay only a few minutes. I promise.'

She looked at him steadily. 'Very well. But *only* a few minutes. It's late. Past your bedtime—or was that part of the act, too?'

'There has been no "act", Charlotte. I gave you no false name, said nothing I did not mean,' he said urgently. 'Please let me explain.'

Charlotte drew away and went into the house. 'I'm curious,' she said as she sat down. 'This house. Who really lives here?'

'No one as yet. It has been prepared for Teresa and Paulinho. They are to be married soon.'

She nodded thoughtfully. 'And if your father hadn't been waiting here this morning, how much longer did you intend keeping up your charade?'

Roberto leaned in the doorway, his fingers loosening his black bow tie. 'You permit? Thank you.' He undid his collar and put the tie in his pocket. 'I wished for one more day. Just one more day.'

'Why?' Charlotte unwound the chiffon wrap and let it trail over the arm of the sofa. 'Why did you want me to think you were just a poor cow-hand, gaucho, whatever? Was it great fun watching me make a fool of myself over the money?'

He eyed her despondently, thrusting a hand through his hair. 'No. I had no wish to humiliate you. My intention——' he hesitated, then went on. 'I wanted to see your reaction to life here, to find out if you liked the *campo*. Not all women care for the isolation. And I suppose I was human enough to want a small revenge myself. So I persuaded the men to dress in their best to meet you, and to ride out with the herd. I wished to impress you with the things tourists like. Also, more than anything else, I wanted you to believe I was just one of the men. The others thought I was *loco*—mad!'

Charlotte's eyes kindled. 'They don't dress like that every day?'

He shrugged. 'Not entirely. The younger ones wear jeans, ride bicycles, drive trucks, but everyone was very happy to—how do you say? Show off?'

She jumped to her feet, seething with indignation. 'Oh, very funny! I hope you all had a really good laugh behind my back!'

Roberto caught her hands in his. 'Please! Do not be angry, *carinha*. I was with you such a short time in England, and that last night my stupid temper made me behave like a barbarian. My punishment was immediate, and enduring. When I returned here all I could think of, dream of, was you.'

Charlotte fought to remain unmoved. 'Is that why you stipulated I must come here in person to close the deal?'

'It was a heaven-sent excuse to get you here, on *minha terra*, my land, my home. I thought I might have been mistaken, that you would be like a fish out of water here.' His eyes glowed. 'But, *carinha*, to have you with me yesterday out there in the *campo*, as if you were born to it, was a dream come true.'

'Then why couldn't you have told me last night who you were?' she demanded. 'We were alone enough. You had plenty of opportunity.'

His hands tightened on hers urgently. 'I wished to ask you a question first, and last night I—I did not dare. I knew I must wait to ask my question in daylight, when we were here with Teresa near by, not out there with no soul for miles.'

A cold little seed of suspicion put up shoots and began to grow inside Charlotte. 'What did you want to ask?'

'While I was still plain Roberto Monteiro, employee of Estancia Velha, owner only of this little house, I wished to ask you to be my wife.' Black, intense eyes locked with startled brown ones. 'I wanted so very much to have you answer *me*, the man, not the son of the *Patrão*.'

'But you didn't ask!'

'No. Because if you, by the grace of God, had said yes to me as I held you in my arms in the night—I could not have kept my promise.'

'What promise?'

'I said that your virginity was a gift only for your husband. If you had promised to marry me I could

not have resisted taking that gift as my right.'
Roberto drew her towards him, but she pushed him
away angrily.

'Wouldn't I have had some say in that? Not that
it matters now. It's all academic anyway.' She shook
her hair back. 'You didn't ask me to marry you,
so my virtue survived the night intact. And now,
even if you *did* ask me you would never be sure,
would you, it it were you or your money I was accepting, Roberto Gaspar Monteiro!'

Colour ebbed away beneath Roberto's tan as he
stared down at her. 'Nevertheless, Charlotte, I *do*
ask you. Will you be my wife, *querida*?'

Charlotte's instinct was to scream, to cry, to
hammer her fists against Roberto's broad chest in
a fury of frustration and misery as her heart and
body urged her to accept, while her mind thrust
them aside. If she accepted his proposal now there
would always be an element of doubt between them.
For the rest of their lives Roberto would never be
sure whether she loved him or the wealth and security he represented. She could have killed him for
making it impossible for her to say yes. Charlotte
raised her head and squared her shoulders, her eyes
glittering darkly at him in fury. Roberto stared
back, his pupils dilating as they dropped to the
quick rise and fall of her breasts.

'Deus!' he said harshly. 'You are everything I
have ever dreamed of. Answer me, Charlotte.' He
took her by the shoulders and shook her a little.
'Speak before I go mad.'

'No!' she hurled at him, then quailed at the look
on his face, as his features sharpened and hardened

until his eyes were like chips of jet set in a bronze mask.

'You will not be my wife?' he asked in a voice so deadly quiet all the hairs rose along Charlotte's spine.

'How can you expect me to be, when you don't even trust me?' she asked unsteadily, and turned her head away, unable to face him.

'I was a fool,' he said. 'I should have taken you last night out there under the stars, when we were just man and woman, when nothing else mattered.' His fingers caught her chin in an iron grip as he turned her face up to his, pain and rage glittering in his eyes. 'I cannot endure the thought of some other man in your bed, your life. We belong, you and I. You know it, Charlotte, you know it!'

'You were the one with the doubts, not me. I came running half-way across the world to you, remember?' Her eyes filled with unwanted tears. 'And now I'm going back where I came from!'

With a stifled sound Roberto dragged her to him and began to kiss her wildly, seizing a handful of hair to hold her head back as his mouth burned its way down her throat to her shoulders on its way to the hollow between her breasts. Charlotte pushed at him violently, and he staggered a little, clutching at her, and the fragile chiffon tore in his grasp. She gave a cry, her hands flying to her breasts, but he caught her wrists, impeding her as the swathed chiffon fell to her waist. Roberto held her arms wide, his eyes drinking in the picture she made, with her hair wild, her eyes flashing fire, her bare, pointing breasts heaving as she twisted and turned and tried to break free. But Roberto Monteiro, accustomed all his adult life to breaking in his own horses, had little trouble in keeping control of one young woman, however much she fought. Charlotte felt her cheeks flame, almost beside herself with angry shame as her nipples hardened visibly in response to the caress of his eyes.

'Let me go!' she panted, but Roberto wasn't even listening, and for the first time in her life Charlotte experienced pure panic as she saw the blind, unreasoning look on his face. 'Please—Roberto—don't . . . You promised——'

His only response was to secure both her wrists in one hand and pull her to him with the other as he bent to take one traitorous nipple in his mouth, pulling gently on it, his coaxing lips sending a fiery dart of sensation right down to her toes. She shook her head wildly and began to fight in earnest, aiming a sharp kick at his shins, but Roberto seemed oblivious to everything but the rage of desire that intensified as his mouth took possession of hers.

Charlotte tore her mouth away. 'Roberto——'

'Fica quieta, amada.' His breath was hot against her mouth as he swung her up easily in his arms and made for the door, utterly impervious to her pummelling and kicking as he strode from the room.

'I'll scream for Teresa——' she panted desperately.

'I will not let you, linda flor,' and his mouth closed on hers as he kicked the bedroom door shut behind him and took her down with him on the bed. Charlotte fought like a tigress, thoroughly frightened at last. Until this moment she had never really believed Roberto would go back on his word. And until now she had always sincerely believed herself equal to stopping any man who tried to take more than she was willing to give. But it was terrifyingly obvious that Roberto intended to have her whether she wanted it or not. And abruptly, right in the thick of the writhing and heat of their struggle a doubt flared in her brain, shocking her rigid. She *did* want it. She stopped fighting, vanquished by her own body's treachery far more easily than by Roberto's superior physical strength.

'*Querida?*' Roberto lifted his head a fraction, but Charlotte couldn't see his face, only feel the heat and purpose of his body, which held her pinned to the bed, one leg thrown over hers, his arms holding her so tightly his onyx shirt studs dug into her skin. She couldn't find words to tell him she was appalled by her own response to the entire situation, that this uncompromising subjugation was, unbelievably, a stimulation in itself. She shuddered, and Roberto groaned softly and began kissing her with seductive gentleness as his hands smoothed and stroked her heated skin, sliding over it in silken caresses that made her body arch involuntarily against his. Suddenly he stiffened.

'Charlotte,' he gasped, and tore himself away, burying his face in the outflung mass of her hair. '*Perdoneme—que demência! Nunca na minha vida...*' He gave an anguished groan and leapt to his feet, leaning his head on his arm against the wall as Charlotte fumbled for the bedside lamp. She lay like a rag-doll, staring at Roberto's back. At some time during their struggle his white dinner jacket had been discarded, and her nails had torn his shirt. She could see his bronzed skin gleaming through the rent in the white material as his shoulders heaved with the effort he was making as he fought for control. At last he squared his shoulders and turned to look at the girl lying on the bed among the tatters of the once-beautiful dress. His face contorted with pain and he closed his eyes, his fists clenching at his side. Belatedly Charlotte drew the woven cotton bedcover over herself.

'I'm decent now,' she said, and he opened his eyes.

'I have no words, Charlotte.' His voice vibrated with disgust. 'Nor excuses. I—I went mad. If it is of any consolation to you, I have never in my life behaved in such a way before.'

Charlotte shrugged. 'But you stopped in the end... No harm was done.'

'No harm!' He came to the edge of the bed, his handsome face bleak with despair. 'Such a *violacão* is not harm?'

Did *violacão* mean rape, wondered Charlotte numbly. She managed a faint, weary smile. 'Oh well, you didn't actually relieve me of—of my famous virtue. Besides, you have only my word for it that it actually exists.'

Roberto looked drawn and haggard in the dim light. 'I know very well that you say the truth.' He hesitated, looking oddly young in his awkwardness. 'What do you want me to do now, Charlotte?'

For one wild moment Charlotte was tempted to tell him, but having just narrowly escaped her first experience of the act of love it seemed unwise to say she wanted him to hold her close and comfort her because her escape, finally, had not been what she wanted after all. She decided to test him a little.

'I think I'd better go home, Roberto. As soon as you can possibly arrange it.' She waited expectantly for his entreaties, utterly sure he would plead with her to stay, repeat his proposal. Instead he inclined his head sombrely and stooped to retrieve his jacket.

'Whatever you wish. *Sempre as seus ordems,* Charlotte.'

She fought to hide her dismay. 'Thank you, Roberto.'

He paused in the doorway. 'I am not sure I can arrange your departure for tomorrow. Perhaps the next day. I will do everything in my power to ensure you stay no longer than you wish.'

Charlotte sat up, securing the bedcover across her breasts. 'Please don't put anyone out. I'll go whenever it's convenient for Senhor Pires to fly me to Port Alegre.'

Roberto bowed formally. 'Then I shall wish you goodnight, Charlotte.'

'Roberto——' She looked away, flushing a little. 'Since I have to stay a little longer, would it be possible for me to go for a short ride in the morning? You don't have to come with me. I'm sure you're very busy and I'm quite used to riding alone.'

'Of course, but it is not advisable for you to ride alone here. If you do not wish for my company I shall send Paulinho to accompany you,' he said brusquely. 'He will be here with the horses at eight.'

Charlotte stared miserably at the door after Robert closed it behind him. That little ruse hadn't gone to plan, either. She had been so sure Roberto would ride with her that she felt like crying her eyes out at the thought of Teresa's *noivo* for company instead. Wearily she got to her feet and stripped off the remains of her dress, rolling it into a ball to hide in her suitcase. She eyed herself in the mirror, surprised to find that apart from her wildly untidy hair, she looked much the same as usual. If Roberto had really made love to her, would there have been a visible difference? she wondered forlornly. She stared resentfully at her reflection. Why the devil didn't you accept when he proposed? she asked it. You love him, don't you? Her reflection nodded. Then would you mind telling me why you said you wanted to go home, you idiot! She said the words out loud, and began to laugh. But laughter turned quickly to tears and she crawled into bed to sob into her pillow until, in the small hours, an idea occurred to her at last which dried her tears like magic. Of course! All she had to do was make sure she stayed at Estancia Velha a little longer that so she could mend matters between herself and Roberto. Charlotte rolled over on her back, linked her hands behind her head in the darkness, and put her mind to work.

CHAPTER TEN

CHARLOTTE was up early next morning, before Teresa had time to prepare breakfast.

'*Bom dia,* Teresa,' she said blithely.

The girl looked at Charlotte's riding-clothes in surprise. '*Bom dia*, Dona Carlota. *A senhora quer café de manha n'a varanda?*'

Charlotte was only too pleased to have her breakfast on the veranda, but ate far less than usual, anxious to get a letter to her parents finished before Paulinho arrived. She had just sealed the envelope when she heard the sound of horses, and saw Paulinho riding towards the house, with Filinha on a leading rein. She smiled at the shy young man, and waved towards the tethering rail.

'*Segura Filinha, faz favor, Paulinho,*' she said carefully, having rehearsed the sentence well during the night. '*Voce pode voltar para casa com minha carta para Inglaterra?*'

The young man nodded, smiling, promising to give her letter to the *Patrão* to send with the day's mail, and to return for Dona Carlota within half an hour to accompany her on her ride. Charlotte watched him out of sight, then fastened on her spurs, put on the flat gaucho hat lent by Roberto and untied Filinha. She swung herself on the horse's back and walked the animal quietly until they were out of earshot of the house, then touched the circular rowels of the spurs to the horse's flanks and

157

put the little grey to the gallop. It would be easy enough to find her way if she followed the direction of the sun. She was fairly sure it was about an hour's ride to the ruins of the Jesuit mission, by which time she would have been well and truly missed and Roberto would come hell for leather after her, and even if they had a grand and glorious fight first they could settle their differences afterwards out here in the *campo* away from everything and everyone.

Charlotte laughed with joy in the blue and gold of the morning, her hair coming loose from its ribbon and streaming out behind her under the hat as she galloped over the great flat ocean of grass. After a while she slowed Filinha to a more leisurely pace, calculating the direction by the sun's position. Certain that the ruins lay straight ahead, somewhere beyond the long white line of fencing stretching to the east, she headed the horse into the sun. It was rather more than an hour before she reached her goal, brimming with excitement and self-congratulation as the piles of stones and graceful arches came into view on the horizon.

'Nearly there, Filinha,' she said, and spurred on her sturdy little mount as they approached the ruins. Her bubbling laugh changed abruptly to a screech of panic as the horse stumbled, shied violently and Charlotte went sailing through the air to land in a crumpled, winded heap on the ground. She struggled to get up, but excruciating pain shot through her leg and she failed, sweat pouring down her face as she saw Filinha rapidly disappearing into the vast blue and green distance. Charlotte moaned in horror, fighting off panic. She felt bruised and battered all over, but the pain in her ankle was intense. Broken, or just sprained? she wondered, and tried to put her weight on it. This was a bad mistake. When she came to again she was lying face down in the grass, feeling hideously sick, and the pain was worse. The sun was very hot, and groggily Charlotte eyed the shade of the nearby ruins. The sensible thing to do was drag herself there until help arrived. And if it doesn't? enquired a voice in her brain. She ignored it, and began the awkward, painful process of moving bit by bit towards the spot where she had drunk coffee so happily with the others only two short days before.

Charlotte was soaked with perspiration and racked with pain by the time she reached cover and lay gasping and exhausted for a long, miserable interval before she could rouse herself sufficiently to remove her sweater. She knew only too well that her boot should come off too, but without help that was impossible. If only she had a knife like Roberto's she could cut if off, she thought, and wadded her sweater into a pillow for her head, tilted her hat over her eyes and tried to rest as best she could. To pass the time she indulged in fantasies where Roberto came galloping up on his horse to the rescue to hold her to his heart and swear never to let her go for the rest of their lives.

God—if only her foot would ease up a little! She bit her lip, badly worried now, because her ankle was swelling inside the boot. Thank heaven they were Laura Monteiro's loose, gaucho-style affairs, rather than her own conventional riding-boots. Charlotte drifted eventually into a feverish, pain-racked doze, then woke with a cry to find the sun beating down on her as it moved overhead. With a groan she crawled into what little shade there was, and settled herself again to wait. After what seemed like hours and hours she heard an aeroplane, the noise growing louder and louder, whirring round and round in her brain, and she heaved herself up on one elbow, shading her eyes with her hand as she saw a helicopter hovering miraculously overhead. Feebly she waved her hat, praying the pilot would see her, and watched, tears of gratitude rolling down her face, as the machine came down to land and two figures came out of it in a crouching run towards her.

The feeling of unreality persisted as she saw it was Roberto who snatched off his helmet as he reached her, followed close behind by Jorge Pires. There was no fantasy at all, however, about the look of black fury in Roberto's eyes as he dropped down beside her.

'*Que loucura!*' he flung at her. 'What madness is this? Do you know what you have done, you little fool? Paulinho is demented because he thinks the *culpa*—the blame, is his. Which it is not. It is yours! When your horse came back without you my father was like a man possessed, and now everyone at Estancia Velha is out searching for you.'

'But...' began Charlotte.

'But nothing! *Escuta*—listen well. Did I not tell you of Amalha and how she died? My father is going through agonies at this moment because he fears I shall find you as he found her!' Almost beside himself with fury and relief, Roberto took her by the hands and dragged her to her feet and Charlotte fainted dead away again with the pain.

This time when she came to she was in Roberto's arms, right enough, but only because he was keeping her secure in the back of the helicopter as Jorge Pires brought the machine down on the green lawn of Estancia Velha. In her daze of pain it seemed to Charlotte that there were people everywhere, exclaiming and running about in all directions as Roberto carried her up the steps to the house. Vaguely she saw Luis Monteiro's face above her, looking lined and years older as he patted her hand, his eyes moist with relief. Robert barked terse directions to the maids as he bore Charlotte up more stairs and into a big, cool room where he laid her unceremoniously on the bed, which was sleigh-shaped and familiar.

'Boots—dirty—spoil the covers,' panted Charlotte.

'N'importa,' he snapped, breathless himself, and shot a look at his father, who was just behind him. *'O medico vem, Pai?'*

'Ja, ja, Roberto. Jorge Pires foi buscar Dr Araujo.'

'I don't need a doctor,' croaked Charlotte. 'I need a drink.'

Roberto scowled blackly at her, then spoke quickly to the maid, who ran from the room. 'The doctor must find out if your ankle is broken, Charlotte. Jorge is bringing him in the helicopter.'

'I'll be fine,' she said fretfully, 'only for God's sake get my boot off—*please*!'

'Hold my hand, *carinha*,' said Luis soothingly, 'and Roberto shall cut off the boot.'

'Oh no! He mustn't—it was your wife's!' Charlotte began to cry, and Roberto cursed quietly as he unsheathed his knife.

'Do not distress yourself,' commanded his father. 'Laura had many such boots. You have only one foot.'

Charlotte grasped his hand tightly as Roberto slit the boot quickly and cleanly and removed it almost in one movement. To her shame Charlotte let out a deep, wrenching groan as the boot came off, and Luis bent to mop her forehead with a large white handkerchief. Roberto took off the other boot with unsteady hands then held a glass of ice-cold water to her lips. Charlotte drank greedily, still holding Luis's hand, then looked up into Roberto's haggard, sweating face and choked back a sob.

'I'm sorry, sorry! Please give my apologies to Paulinho, and to Teresa too. I never intended to worry you all to death. And Filinha—is she all right?' she added anxiously.

'Yes,' said Roberto, staring down at Charlotte's dusty, tear-streaked face. '*Pai*, would you be so kind as to leave us for a moment, please.'

'*Não, meu filho*' said Luis Monteiro with authority. 'Let the child be washed and clothed more comfortably. Also I believe Dr Araujo should see her before you begin questioning her.'

Roberto seemed about to argue when the sound of the helicopter interrupted him. '*Muito bem*. The doctor comes now, I think.'

Charlotte was put through a very harrowing half-hour while, in the presence of Figenia and Sonia, the two maids, Dr Araujo, a brisk, kind man, examined the patient for injuries and probed the injured ankle, pronouncing it badly sprained but not broken.

'You were very fortunate, young lady!' His eyes twinkled as he said goodbye. 'You will soon learn not to take liberties with the *campo*, Miss Charlotte.'

It would hardly be necessary, thought Charlotte in misery, as the two sympathetic girls removed her clothes and washed her with great care. After this stupid escapade it was more than likely Roberto would want to pack her off home as soon as he possibly could. Figenia slid one of Charlotte's own lawn nightgowns over her head, administered the painkillers left by the doctor and beckoned Sonia from the room, leaving Charlotte staring up at the canopy, wondering if Roberto had brought the bed back with him from Presteigne House. She bit her lip as her ankle gave her a sharp reminder of its presence, tears trickling from the corners of her eyes as she thought of her confidence earlier on. Her escape on Filinha had seemed like such an adventure, destined to bring about a happy ending so neatly. Instead she had set Estancia Velha in uproar, given Luis Monteiro a terrible shock, and probably alienated Roberto for ever, by the look on his face when he found her. The thoughts went on and on chasing themselves in never-ending sequence in her mind until she fell asleep at last from sheer exhaustion.

Charlotte woke slowly, her eyes puzzled as they took in the strange room, then a twinge from her ankle told her where she was and why she was there and she sighed shakily, suddenly desperate for the sound of her mother's voice.

'That was a very big sigh, *carinha*!'

Charlotte turned her head sharply to see Roberto, in crisp white shirt and linen trousers, lounging in a wicker chair near the bed. 'I—I didn't realise you were there,' she said, embarrassed.

'My father does not approve,' said Roberto lightly. 'He does not think it right for me to be alone with you in your bedroom.'

His father was right, thought Charlotte, remembering the night before, and Roberto interpreted the look with accuracy, waving a hand at the door, which stood wide open.

'All the world may look on if it wishes, as you can see.' He got up, looking down at her. 'Now, Charlotte, would you like something to drink?'

'Yes, please,' She struggled to sit up as he poured fresh lemonade from a glass jug, and Roberto put down the glass and lifted her gently, settling pillows behind her.

'Can you hold the glass yourself?'

She smiled a little. 'I sprained my ankle. My hands are fine.' She drank deeply, nerving herself up for the explanation she knew he had a right to expect. 'Roberto, I really am deeply sorry for all the trouble I caused.'

He nodded thoughtfully. 'I will not say it was nothing. Everyone was wild with anxiety when Filinha came back without you, though before that, of course, Paulinho had been out for some time looking for you.'

'But you weren't,' said Charlotte.

'No.' He smiled at her. 'I had ridden with my father to inspect some fences Jorge Pires had reported broken. As soon as I learned you were missing I rode back to collect the helicopter. It is the most effective method of searching for anything lost, from stray calves to missing English visitors.' His eyes mocked her and Charlotte bit her lip. 'Alas,' he added soberly, 'we did not own a helicopter—or an aeroplane—when Amalha ran away. And this time I would not allow my father to join in the search for you.'

'Why not?'

'I was much afraid of what I would find.' His voice roughened. '*Deus me livre*, Charlotte—what possessed you to do such a senseless thing?'

Charlotte looked at him in silence for a while, then in a bleak, tired voice, told him about her plan, conscious now of how childish it seemed. 'I thought it was such a simple way to mend our own private fences, so to speak,' she finished, and turned away, unable to meet his eyes. 'Instead of which I seem to have made things a hundred times worse.'

Roberto was quiet for a long, testing interval. 'Tell me, Charlotte,' he said at last. 'What were your thoughts as you lay out there in the sun alone? Did you think that history was repeating itself?'

She turned back to him, surprised. 'No. Never. I knew you would find me in time. After all, I'd hurt my ankle, not broken my neck like poor Amalha.'

'You were most fortunate I did not break it for you.' Roberto's eyes kindled. 'I was dangerously close to it when I found you. I was very angry.'

'I could see that.' She smiled faintly. 'Who could blame you? But I must admit the helicopter was a sad disappointment. I expected you to come galloping to my rescue on a big white horse and carry me off to safety in your arms, you know.'

Roberto threw back his head and roared with laughter, much to the surprise of Luis Monteiro, who came into the room at that point.

'Charlotte must be better!' Luis Monteiro's handsome eyes were bright with relief as he bent to take one of her hands. 'How do you feel, *chica*?'

'A little tired and sore, and very, *very* silly and embarrassed.' Charlotte smiled up at him ruefully. 'Please forgive me, Senhor Monteiro.'

'How could I not?' he said simply, and patted her hand. 'And now, my child, I think we shall put a call through to your parents, and inform them your return home must be delayed a little, *não é*?'

Charlotte was touched by his thoughtfulness, even though later on the call home proved very unsettling in her current state of weakness. At the sound of her mother's familiar, calm accents Charlotte was hard put to it not to howl like a baby, and only the thought of Janine's disapproval of such gauche behaviour kept her from doing so. Nevertheless an occasional wobble in her voice must have managed to percolate through several thousand miles of telephone line.

'*Doucement, bébé,*' exhorted her mother. 'Do not upset yourself. *C'est incroyable*—first Jake with a broken leg, now you with a sprained ankle. I shall keep a very close eye on William, I think, in case he also tries to break some part of himself.'

Charlotte laughed unsteadily and sent her love to her little brother. 'And *Maman*, tell Dad the contract is all signed and sealed.'

'He knows, *chérie*. Both Roberto and his father spoke with Jake first before you were put through to me.'

'Oh.' Charlotte felt surprised. 'Fine. So I'll be home as soon as I can stand on my foot——'

'You need not hurry, Charlotte. All is well here. And Roberto assures us you are welcome at Estancia Velha as long as you wish to stay.'

Like for the rest of my life? Charlotte refrained from shocking her mother with that particular question and said '*Au'voir* then, *Maman*. I miss you.'

'And I miss you,*chérie*,' said her mother fondly. '*Au'voir, p'tite.*'

For the rest of the evening Charlotte was suffering enough reaction to her adventures to be glad to lie in the beautiful bed and eat her dinner from a tray. To her amusement, although Roberto spent a great deal of the time with her, the bedroom door remained wide open and Figenia, she was informed, would spend the night in the adjoining dressing-room.

'Is this the master bedroom?' Charlotte asked when Roberto joined her after dinner.

'It was when my mother came here as a bride. After she died my father could never bear to sleep here again without her.' His eyes met hers. 'Amalha and I had a different room at the back of the house, also with a dressing-room, fortunately, since I slept in it far more than in the *cama de casal*. I have occupied the same rooms ever since. I did not feel the same sense of loss as my father on the death of my wife. I felt only relief to be free. Though God knows I would not have chosen to gain my freedom in such a way.'

'No,' agreed Charlotte quietly. She gestured towards the canopy. 'Is this your grandmother's bed?'

'No. It is a copy my father had made here for my mother. The bed at Presteigne House is a genuine antique, acquired by some ancestor of mine.'

'This one is a marvellous copy,' Charlotte stretched a little, easing her aching body.

'You have pain?' he asked instantly.

'No more than before—and certainly no more than I deserve.' She looked at him pleadingly. 'Have you forgiven me, Roberto?'

'Between you and me, *querida*, there is no question of forgiveness, am I right?' Roberto rose to stand by the bed, looking down at her with tenderness in the eyes that had been so furious when he found her.

'Then you're not angry with me any more?'

His eyes gleamed suddenly. 'I might ask you the same question.'

Charlotte smiled at him, suddenly soaringly happy. 'You were right, Roberto. The questions are superfluous.'

'Come, my son,' said Luis Monteiro from the doorway. 'It is time to leave our charming invalid to sleep.' He scrutinised his son's face. 'You, also, Roberto, need sleep, I think. The day has been tiring for all.'

'*E verdade,*' said Roberto with feeling, and turned stern eyes on Charlotte. 'Can you be trusted to stay here safely all night, Miss Mercer? Or may we expect to learn at breakfast that you have decided to try to fly off in the helicopter this time?'

'No way,' she assured him. 'I know my limitations.'

'I trust your adventure today has not spoiled your stay at Estancia Velha, Charlotte,' said Luis Monteiro. 'I have been much troubled that your time out there alone in the *campo* may have given you a fear of it.'

'Definitely not,' said Charlotte without reservation. 'My only regret was that I let go of Filinha. Otherwise I would have ridden back, ankle or no ankle.'

She was rewarded by a glowing look from Roberto, and a nod of satisfied approval from his father.

'*Muito bom.* You are a brave girl.' He turned to his son. 'Come, Roberto. We must let this child sleep.'

Roberto complied at once, kissing Charlotte's hand, and leaving her to Figenia to settle her in for the night.

It was almost a week before Charlotte could walk unaided, a week spent in resting during the day on the veranda, and in the evenings on one of the comfortable hide sofas in the *sala*. She hobbled about with the aid of a stick at first, but the ankle mended quickly, too quickly for her taste, since recovery would mean no further excuse to linger at Estancia Velha. Roberto was as attentive as she could wish during the time he could spare to spend with her, but his duties on the *estancia* took him away from the house for most of the daylight hours, and it was left to Luis Monteiro to keep her company each day until the evening. Charlotte grew very fond of him as she came to know him better. Since his accident he had become an avid reader, and delighted in discussions with Charlotte on literature and art, and once he realised his guest was eager to know about his dead wife, talked at length about his beloved Laura.

'She came with her parents to stay with her Monteiro relatives in Santa Catarina when she was a young girl,' he said, his fine eyes dreamy with reminiscence. 'They were connections of mine— Laura was, you know, a distant cousin. I was invited to a party given for her, and was obliged to fight off several of my countrymen for the privilege of a dance with her.'

Charlotte smiled at him affectionately. 'So you were like my father. You fell in love at first sight.'

Luis laughed. '*Sim. I* did. Laura, however, had many suitors at home in Yorkshire. I had to work hard to persuade her I was the only man for her.' He sighed. 'She did not regret choosing me, I know, which is a comfort now I am without her.'

Charlotte put a hand on his. 'You must miss her.'

'I do, *carinha*.' Luis smiled at her. 'Just as your father will miss you when you marry. More, perhaps, than most fathers, since you work for him.'

Charlotte shrugged. 'Now Dad has William to follow him in the firm eventually he won't mind so much. Besides, no one is indispensable. Someone else could do what I do without too much trouble.'

She was sketching as she talked. Roberto had sent to Porto Alegre for charcoal and large sheets of cartridge paper, and from her chair on the veranda she drew everything she could see: the eucalyptus and acacias clustering near the house, a glimpse of the great *sala* through the open doors, and one day Roberto tethered Filinha nearby so that Charlotte could sketch the little horse as it grazed in the shade. Another time, while Luis dozed after lunch, she drew his aquiline profile with its crown of curling hair, and he accepted the drawing later with delight, showing it to Roberto with pride as they sat over drinks before dinner that night.

'I am jealous,' declared Roberto. 'Will you draw me also, Charlotte?'

She coloured a little, reluctant to admit that she had already drawn his face several times in private, never satisfied that she had done justice to his handsome features. 'If you like,' she said, feeling unaccountably shy.

Shy! she thought with derision, in bed later that night. Roberto Monteiro has seen you half-naked, made love to you far more thoroughly than any man has ever done, and yet he makes you feel shy! Ben Ackroyd and company would never believe it of the girl they thought of as the boss's efficient, no-nonsense daughter. Charlotte smiled wryly in the darkness. She had undergone some kind of metamorphosis since the day Roberto Monteiro met her eye across his grandmother's grave. Now she hardly knew where she was, or how to describe their relationship. Since her adventure in the *campo* Roberto had been attentive and kind, but downright impersonal, she thought wistfully. A bit different from the wild, demanding lover of that unforgettable night. It was a sobering thought to realise that although she was now able quite literally to stand on her own two feet, in another way her esteemed independence seemed oddly unimportant these days. Not to put too fine a point on it, she wanted nothing more than to spend the rest of her life right here in Estancia Velha as Roberto Monteiro's wife, but it gave her no comfort at all to remember that he had made her the requisite proposal of marriage, because so far he'd made no move at all to repeat it.

CHAPTER ELEVEN

AFTER a restless night Charlotte was roused earlier than usual next morning. When Figenia brought her breakfast tray there was a note on it from Roberto asking Charlotte if she would like to see the *domadores*, the horsebreakers, in action.

'I have been breaking in a new colt to replace my faithful Relâmpago,' he wrote. 'This morning he is to have his first experience of the saddle.'

Charlotte was out of bed and dressed in a flash, swallowing her coffee as she tied back her hair. She made her way downstairs as fast as her ankle allowed, and found Luis Monteiro waiting for her, smiling in welcome.

'*Bom dia,* Charlotte. You slept well?'

'Good morning, *Senhor Patrão*. I slept fairly well.' Charlotte looked about her eagerly. 'Where's Roberto?'

'With the others, *carinha*.' He held out his hand. 'I have been ordered to escort you. Is your ankle strong enough to walk that far, Charlotte?'

She assured him it was, and accompanied him towards the *curral*, the railed enclosure beyond the vine-covered outbuildings near by, where she could hear men's voices and the sound of a horse whickering.

'How do they tame a horse?' asked Charlotte with some misgivings. Her experience of horses was confined to the stable-bred hacks in Prestleigh, animals which had little in common with the tough, rough-coated descendants of wild mustangs used on Estancia Velha.

Luis patted her hand reassuringly. 'It is a long process, very gradual, with gentle handling over many months. Roberto has been very patient with this colt, taking much time with it. Diablinho is the creature's name, because he has truly been a little devil, more difficult than most, but with a great spirit. Very different from Roberto's beloved Relâmpago.'

'Relâmpago?' asked Charlotte.

'It means "lightning", *carinha*.' Luis sighed. 'Roberto was heartbroken when Relâmpago broke a leg the day before you arrived. He shot the horse himself, and shut himself up in his room for hours afterwards.'

Charlotte's eyes widened. So that was the bereavement which had kept Roberto from meeting her in Porto Alegre—a horse, not a relative. As they grew close she saw a group of men milling round a stout wooden post in the centre of the *curral*, where a horse was tethered by a length of the plaited leather rope which was coiled at every gaucho's saddle. Some of the men were on horseback, others on foot, and Roberto, unaware of Charlotte's presence, was speaking soothingly in the animal's laid-back ear.

Luis held Charlotte firmly by the arm. 'Go no closer, *chica*.'

She stood still, her eyes riveted on Roberto as, very gently, talking all the time to the horse, he eased the sandwich of leather pads and blankets on to the animal's back. At once the horse gave a scream of terror and tried to buck the offending weight off, but the man ready on the other side hung on, dodging out of the way of the hobbled rear hooves as Roberto rapidly secured the saddle in place, then gentled the trembling, sweating animal into eventual calm. It stood, head down, still trembling, pulling slightly on the rope, and all the time Roberto kept talking quietly into the animal's ears in a monotonous, soothing litany of reassurance.

Charlotte gripped Luis's arm tightly as one of the men cautiously removed the hobble from the horse's back legs and Roberto vaulted into the saddle, saying '*Liga!*' to the other man, who untied the rope as ordered and the horse was free, immediately trying its utmost to rid itself of this new added burden. Charlotte bit back a cry as Roberto thrust his feet into the stirrups and hung on to the reins for dear life, leaning far back in the saddle as the horse bucked its back feet in the air, nose down, then reared up, standing on its back legs while Roberto fought for control, gripping with his knees, every sinew straining as the horse came down again and careered off wildly, mane flying as it circled the *curral* at breakneck speed, the men scattering in all directions before it.

Charlotte could hardly bear to look, yet at the same time could not tear her eyes away from the spectacle of man and horse bound up in a struggle for mastery, the animal gradually losing the battle as the superb rider remained in the saddle, ignoring all the tricks the colt tried to throw him off.

'*Muito bem feito,*' muttered Luis beside her, his eyes glowing with pride as his son gradually won the upper hand over the colt. 'He rides like a centaur, *não é*?'

Charlotte was too tense to answer, her heart still in her throat as she watched the horse begin to tire of its stampede. The circle of grinning, triumphant faces watched the son of the *Patrão* with pride and admiration, and suddenly one of the younger ones threw his hat in the air and Charlotte let out an involuntary cry of protest. Roberto looked up sharply and lost the reins as the horse shied again and its rider sailed through the air much as Charlotte had done only a few days before. The horse's flying hooves caught Roberto's body a glancing blow as he lay winded, and there was instant uproar as some men ran to him, others to catch the horse, and Charlotte tore herself away from Luis and sped like an arrow to Roberto, ducking through the rails of the *curral* to throw herself on her knees by his side, elbowing men out of the way without ceremony in her frantic need to know if he was hurt.

'Roberto!' she cried, and bent over him in a frenzy of anxiety. She sat in the dust and heaved him across her knees, resting his head on her lap, and Roberto's thick black lashes lifted, his dazed eyes staring up into Charlotte's in wonder. 'Are you all right?' she demanded, and for answer his arm shot up and pulled her down to him.

'I am now,' he muttered against her lips and kept her where she was, almost bent double over him, his mouth giving her all the reassurance she needed. Charlotte kissed him back fiercely, oblivious of the grinning group of men, who melted away discreetly, leaving Senhor Roberto to ministrations he obviously preferred to any they could supply.

'Darling—are you hurt? Tell me!' demanded Charlotte when she could speak, and ran searching fingers through his hair, which was matted with dust and sweat. Roberto shook his head, his eyes dancing as she ran her hands over his ribs and down his legs in her hurry to make sure he was in one piece.

'*Querida,*' he said huskily, catching her hands. 'If you wish to continue like this, do you not think it better we retire indoors where we have less audience?'

Charlotte raised her head, not in the least perturbed that Luis Monteiro and Jorge Pires were watching them with interest, and she sprang up after the latter came hurrying to assist as Roberto got to his feet.

'*Nada queibrada?*' asked Jorge, as the *Patrão* joined them.

'*Não, obrigado.* Nothing broken.' Roberto put an arm out to pull Charlotte close. 'Nevertheless I shall need constant nursing for a long time in order to recover from the shock.'

'*Que bobo!*' said Luis mildly. 'You stay on the horse at the most difficult moment, then come off once the colt has acknowledged you as master!'

'I caught sight of Charlotte,' admitted Roberto, grinning, and tightened his arm as she tried to move away.

'A sight to distract any man,' agreed his father. 'Come, Jorge, let us see that all is well with the colt, and leave my son to Charlotte's care.' He smiled at the dishevelled girl. 'It is of no use now to protest that Roberto's well being is of no interest to you, *carinha*, since you have demonstrated only too plainly to all the world that it is!'

Charlotte walked back to the house with Roberto in a silence which he broke only when they were inside and alone in the great sala.

'Now,' he said imperiously. 'Demonstrate this interest to me, *querida*. I need very badly to hear you say you care for me.'

Charlotte buried her face against his shoulder as his arms closed round her. 'Oh, I care, Roberto Monteiro. I can hardly deny it when I made such a fuss out there.' She shivered and hugged him closer. 'I thought the horse would kick you in the head.' She tipped her head back to look into his dusty, triumphant face. 'Are you sure you're not hurt?'

'A trifling kick in the ribs—a small price to pay for the knowledge you love me, Charlotte.' He kissed her cheek delicately. 'Because you do, *amada*, am I not right?'

She sighed and turned her face so that their lips met, clung, then parted sufficiently for her to say, 'I love you, Roberto Monteiro, so much that I've been dreading the thought of leaving you to go away.'

His eyes dwelt on her face possessively. 'When you go I shall go too.'

'To Prestleigh?' Her eyes widened.

'*Sim*, to Prestleigh.' His smile was triumphant. 'I have already asked your father's permission to marry you.'

'Oh, *have* you!' Charlotte stepped back, eyed him militantly. 'You haven't asked *me*!'

'I was waiting for the right moment to present itself.' He laughed joyously and took her hands. 'Not as romantic as I would have wished, when we are both filthy and I reek of horse—nevertheless...' He went down on one knee, the laughter fading from his eyes. 'Will you be my wife, Charlotte? And give me sons—daughters too, and let me love you for the rest of our lives?'

Charlotte looked about her, hunted, afraid the maids would come in. 'Yes, yes, only please get up.'

He leapt to his feet and took her in his arms, rubbing his cheek against hers. *'Meu amor!'*

'You still haven't said you love me,' she felt obliged to point out.

'Have I not?' He drew away and laid a hand on his heart. *'Eu te adoro, eu te amo e eu te quero— até o fim de minha vida.'* He drew her close. 'Do I need to translate? I adore you, Charlotte Mercer, I love you and I want you—*Deus,* how I want you! And I shall do so until the end of my life, and after.'

Charlotte's smile was incandescent. 'No translation was necessary. I know what you meant.'

'Because it was my heart talking to yours,' said Roberto, in a tone that melted her bones. He held her close and kissed her without passion, as though it was the sealing of a bond between them, then held her away firmly. 'And now, *linda flor*, let us go upstairs and have a bath.'

'Together, Senhor Monteiro?' she mocked, as they went upstairs, arms about each other.

Roberto closed his eyes in suffering. 'Do not say such things, *bruxa*! My patience will be sorely tried as it is until we marry. Do not, I implore, make it more difficult for me with such words!'

'Sorry, darling.' Charlotte hugged him close at the top of the stairs, then broke away reluctantly to enter the master bedroom alone. 'Shall we share this room, Roberto, when we're married?'

'If it is what you want, Charlotte.' He took her hand and kissed it. 'You may sleep in whatever room in the house you choose—so long as I sleep there with you.'

Prestleigh had always taken a great interest in Jake Mercer. He was an interesting man, everyone agreed, approving strongly of his progress from bricklayer at eighteen to property tycoon by his late forties. Local opinion had been a bit mixed about his marriage to a French lass, but she was a right sensible lady, Janine Mercer, and not only had she presented Jake with a stunner of a daughter, but proved him capable of fathering a little lad when most of his contemporaries were thinking of grandchildren. And now here he was, turning the Presteigne estate into the Presteigne Golf and Country Club, and to cap it all young Charlotte was marrying old Mrs Presteigne's grandson and taking off to Brazil to live on some kind of ranch. A bit of smack in the eye for Ben Ackroyd, this last, was the general opinion. The wedding, Prestleigh agreed unanimously, was the finest the town had ever witnessed, champagne flowing like water. It was even a sunny day. Trust Jake Mercer to have luck even with the weather. Janine Mercer looked so lovely it was hard to believe she was young William's mother, let alone the bride's, and that Roberto Monteiro wasn't half a good-looking chap. For that matter so was his dad. Quite a few people remembered him from his wedding to Laura Presteigne. Seemed these Monteiro chaps liked Yorkshire lasses.

There were sighs from the female wedding guests as Roberto Monteiro kissed his bride at the altar, and a few of the men nudged each other as Ben Ackroyd tried to make out he was pleased as punch over the whole thing. There were sly grins as one wag expressed the opinion that Ben was hardly likely to get very far with Jake Mercer's new assistant, because this time Jake had taken on the son of one of his business cronies. And there was some surprise about Charlotte's decision to get cracking with her new life straight off instead of going to Venice or the Greek islands, like other recent Prestleigh honeymoon couples. But she'd always been a sensible lass, it was agreed. This Monteiro chap was a right lucky man.

'So you fly a plane as well,' commented Charlotte, as they took off from Porto Alegre on the last leg of their journey.

Roberto nodded, smiling. 'You are nervous with me at the controls?'

'No.' Which was perfectly true. By this stage Charlotte had supreme confidence in her husband's skill at whatever task he undertook, and sat relaxed and happy during the flight. She looked down proprietorially as the grassland rolled below them, her eyes sparkling as she saw the first of the Monteiro herds on the horizon. 'We're almost home, Roberto.'

His eyes were tender as they glanced briefly at her happy face. 'I am glad that you think of Estancia Velha as "home", *amada*.'

'Oh I'll get homesick for Prestleigh now and then, darling. You'd better be prepared for that. But, in essence, from now on home is where you are. Where *we* are; together.'

'It is necessary for me to concentrate on the landing,' said Roberto with suppressed feeling, 'otherwise I would express my gratitude in no uncertain way for such a gratifying sentiment.'

They arrived to a tumultuous welcome from men dressed in their best gaucho outfits, women and children smiling and vociferous as Roberto lifted his bride from the aircraft. It was some time before the couple could break away to make for the house, where Roberto picked his bride up with grave ceremony and carried her into the *sala*, kissing her lovingly, to the delight of the smiling maids, before setting her down.

'How long do you need?' he asked, as their luggage was brought in.

'Give me thirty minutes to shower and change, then I'll be ready to eat,' said Charlotte as they went upstairs, and Roberto kissed her cheek and went off to his old room to change, leaving her in the master bedroom with the maids. She chatted to them happily in her fragmented, erratic Portuguese as they unpacked her clothes, and exactly half an hour later, showered, changed, her hair brushed and shining, Charlotte joined Roberto for their welcome-home meal at the rosewood table, tucking into grilled steaks and suckling pig with an enthusiasm much approved by Figenia and Sonia, as they brought out the iced cake baked in honour of the occasion. Shortly afterwards Charlotte smiled up at her husband.

'Ready when you are, my love.'

Roberto led his bride out on to the veranda and knelt at her feet to buckle on her spurs, then handed her the familiar flat hat, pulled his own lower over his eyes and went with her to the *curral*, where Jorge Pires waited with Filinha and the now docile Diablinho. The horses were hung with extra bedrolls and provisions, and Diablinho gave a whicker of welcome to greet his master. Roberto patted his neck and spoke to him softly, then gave Charlotte a leg up on Filinha and swung himself up on Diablinho, with a word of thanks to Jorge. Charlotte joined in the goodbyes as the horses set off, her face flushed and happy as she smiled at Roberto.

'We have two hours of daylight, *amada*,' he told her, 'So let us not linger. It is one hour to the place where you wish to spend the night, and I shall need the other hour to start the fire and prepare our beds.'

As they set off towards the descending sun, alone in the landscape of grass and sky, Charlotte took in a deep breath of utter contentment.

'You are happy, *querida*?' asked Roberto.

'Very.'

He laughed, and waved a hand about him. 'Few brides would choose such a setting for—for——'

'Their wedding night?' She grinned at him like an urchin. 'But then, dearest heart, not many husbands would have waited with such exemplary patience!'

'I have waited,' agreed Roberto ruefully, 'but not,
I confess, with patience. It has been difficult, but
I have survived.'

'São Roberto; saint indeed,' teased Charlotte,
and pointed in sudden excitement to trees in the
distance. 'Isn't that the place, Roberto?'

'*Não, senhora.* We have several kilometres yet.
You are not too tired?' he asked anxiously. 'If so
we shall make camp here.'

'No indeed. It must be that special place where
we spent our first night together.' Charlotte held
firm, and Roberto laughed indulgently.

'You shall spend your wedding night exactly
where you wish, *minha linda esposa.*'

'OK, then. So let's get a move on!'

It was a little more than an hour later when they
finally reached the familiar spot near the tree-
fringed stream. But this time a fire had been laid
for them in advance, with plenty of spare wood
stacked near by. Extra sheepskins hung rolled up
in a nearby tree and there were pillows in a water-
proof bag near the kindling. 'This time we shall be
a little more comfortable,' said Roberto as he lifted
Charlotte down from the horse.

'And this time I can actually help. Last time I
was an aching bag of bones!'

'I am grateful,' he said, poker-faced, 'that things
are different tonight.'

Charlotte grinned at him and busied herself with
spreading sheepskins for their bed. The fire was
soon blazing, water boiling for coffee, the horses
unsaddled and grazing peacefully together, and
Charlotte curled up on the nest of blankets, her
head on Roberto's shoulder, his arms close about

her as the flames grew bright against the darkening sky. They talked desultorily of the wedding and the journey and the new bull due to arrive at the Estancia, then Roberto disentangled himself and went over to the stream, returning with a bottle of champagne.

'How clever,' said Charlotte, laughing. 'Did you order that in advance too?'

'For this night only,' he stated firmly. 'In future I fear you will have no such luxuries out here in the *campo*. Tonight—tonight is different.'

Charlotte looked up at him as he poured the wine. 'I'll drink to that. To us, Roberto.'

'To us,' he echoed, his eyes holding hers as they toasted each other. When the champagne was finished he built the fire higher then lay down on the blankets and held up his arms. 'I fear I have no more patience, *querida*. Come to me now, Charlotte, I implore. I can wait no longer.'

It was much later, when the fire was low and the stars luminous in the velvet darkness, that Charlotte finally stirred in her husband's arms.

'I'm so glad, Roberto.'

He kissed her with a new possessiveness. 'Why are you glad, *amada*?'

'That I waited—that *we* waited until now.'

Roberto's arms tightened about her, and he buried his face in her hair. 'There were times when I felt I could wait no more, when all I could think of was having you in my arms like this, your body——' he breathed in unsteadily, 'your so beautiful body close to mine. But, yes, *querida*, I am very glad we waited. It has been so very much worth the waiting.'

'I didn't make you wait out of sheer whim, you know.' Charlotte reached up a hand to his face in the darkness. 'When you spoke of my—my inexperience as a gift for my husband it seemed so right. Antiquated perhaps, but exactly right for you and me. Particularly since...' She halted, reluctant to spoil the moment.

'Particularly since my first wedding night was one of disillusion!' Roberto got up to feed the fire, then let himself down beside Charlotte again, drawing her close. 'It was your intention also, was it not, Charlotte, for tonight to be different in every way for us, that we make love here under the stars the first time instead of in a bed as most lovers do?'

'Yes,' she confessed. 'I wanted a night we could remember and look back on with love and joy.'

Roberto kissed her hard, his hands sliding beneath the blankets to caress her. *'Meu amor,'* he said huskily. 'No man is more fortunate than I.' He put his lips close to her ear. 'But you speak as though this night were over, *carinha*. Yet it is a long, long time until dawn. I have only just begun to enjoy this wedding gift you have given me.'

'Oh,' said Charlotte.

'Yes, oh!' he teased. 'How sophisticated you look, *querida*, and how naïve you really are. And how very seductive I find such naïveté.'

'I'm not at all naïve,' declared Charlotte breathlessly, restless beneath his coaxing hands. 'I'd have you know I'm an experienced married woman...'

'Who will be a great deal more experienced by morning,' muttered her husband.

'Good,' said the blushing bride. 'I've a lot of time to make up, remember.'

Roberto's delighted laughter mingled with his bride's, then their laughter died away into silence broken only by endearments meant exclusively for each other, unheard by another soul in the vast, starlit expanse of the pampas of Rio Grande do Sul.

Harlequin Presents®

Coming Next Month

Available in August wherever paperback books are sold, or through
Harlequin Reader Service:

In the U.S.
901 Fuhrmann Blvd.
P.O. Box 1397
Buffalo, N.Y. 14240-1397

In Canada
P.O. Box 603
Fort Erie, Ontario
L2A 5X3

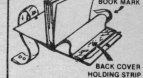

Harlequin Regency Romance™

Romance the way it was *always* meant to be!

The time is 1811, when a Regent Prince rules the empire. The place is London, the glittering capital where rakish dukes and dazzling debutantes scheme and flirt in a dangerously exciting game. Where marriage is the passport to wealth and power, yet every girl hopes secretly for love....

Welcome to Harlequin Regency Romance where reading is an adventure and romance is *not* just a thing of the past! Two delightful books a month.

Available wherever Harlequin Books are sold.

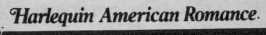